BAD GIRLFRIEND

BILLIONAIRES CLUB #13

ELISE FABER

BAD GIRLFRIEND
BY ELISE FABER
Newsletter sign-up

BAD GIRLFRIEND
Copyright © 2021 Elise Faber
Print ISBN-13: 978-1-63749-030-3
Ebook ISBN-13: 978-1-63749-029-7
Cover Art by Jena Brignola

BILLIONAIRE'S CLUB

Bad Night Stand

Bad Breakup

Bad Husband

Bad Hookup

Bad Divorce

Bad Fiancé

Bad Boyfriend

Bad Blind Date

Bad Wedding

Bad Engagement

Bad Bridesmaid

Bad Swipe

Bad Girlfriend

Bad Best Friend

BILLIONAIRE'S CLUB CAST OF CHARACTERS

Heroes and Heroines:

Abigail Roberts (Bad Night Stand) — founding member of the Sextant, hates wine, loves crocheting

Jordan O'Keith (Bad Night Stand) — Heather's brother, former owner of RoboTech

Cecilia (CeCe) Thiele (Bad Breakup) — former nanny to Hunter, talented artist

Colin McGregor (Bad Breakup) — Scottish duke, owner of McGregor Enterprises

Heather O'Keith (Bad Husband) — CEO of RoboTech, Jordan's sister

Clay Steele (Bad Husband) — Heather's business rival, CEO of Steele Technologies

Kay (Bad Date) — romance writer, hates to be stood up

Garret Williams (Bad Date) — former rugby player

Rachel Morris (Bad Hookup) — Heather's assistant, super-powers include being ultra-organized

Sebastian (Bas) Scott (Bad Hookup) — Devon Scott's brother, Clay's assistant

Rebecca (Bec) Darden (Bad Divorce) — kickass lawyer, New York roots

Luke Pearson (Bad Divorce) — Southern gentleman, CEO Pearson Energies

Seraphina Delgado (Bad Fiancé) — romantic to the core, looks like a bombshell, but even prettier on the inside

Tate Connor (Bad Fiancé) — tech genius, scared to be burned by love

Lorelai (Bad Text) — drunk texts don't make her happy

Logan Smith (Bad Text) — former military, sometimes drunk texts are for the best

Kelsey Scott (Bad Boyfriend) — Bas and Devon's sister, engineer at RoboTech, brilliant

Tanner Pearson (Bad Boyfriend) — Bas and Devon's childhood friend, photographer

Trix Donovan (Bad Blind Date) — Heather's sister, Jordan's half-sister, nurse who worked in war zones, poverty-stricken areas, and abroad for almost a decade

Jet Hansen (Bad Blind Date) — a doctor Trix worked with

Molly Miller (Bad Wedding) — owner of Molly's, a kickass bakery in San Francisco

Jackson Davis (Bad Wedding) — Molly's ex-fiancé

Kate McLeod (Bad Engagement) — Kelsey's college friend, advertiser extraordinaire, loves purple and Hermione Granger

Jaime Huntingon (Bad Engagement) — vet, does excellent man-bun

Heidi Greene (Bad Bridesmaid) — science, organization, and *Twilight* nerd

Brad Huntington (Bad Bridesmaid) — travel junkie, dreamy hazel eyes, hidden sweet side

Ben Bradford (Bad Swipe) — quiet, brooding, had a thing for golden retrievers
Stef McKay (Bad Swipe) — lab assistant, dog lover, klutzy to the extreme
Tammy Huntington (Bad Girlfriend) — allergic to relationships
Fletcher King (Bad Girlfriend) — has a thing for smart, sassy women

Additional Characters:

George O'Keith — Jordan's dad
Hunter O'Keith — Jordan's nephew
Bridget McGregor — Colin's mom
Lena McGregor — Colin's sister
Bobby Donovan — Heather's half and Trix's full brother
Frances and Sugar Delgado — Sera's parents
Devon Scott — Kels and Bas's brother
Becca Scott — Kels and Bas's sister in law
Fred — the bestest golden retriever in the world
Sir Fuzzy McFeatherston aka The Fuzz — Jaime and Kate's pet rooster

ONE

Tammy

Are you really breaking up with me via text?

TAMMY WINCED as she read the text message and started to set down her cell.

But it vibrated again.

While I'm in your bathroom?

She winced. Okay, so her timing wasn't ideal.

Sighing, she tugged the covers back and pulled on her robe. Her frumpy, holey, old flannel robe that absolutely dwarfed her and was so unappealing that it had run off more than her fair share of men.

Which was why she only pulled it out for very special occasions.

Her period when she felt horrible and crampy and

exhausted and just wanted to veg on the couch and pretend that her uterus wasn't shredding itself to pieces.

The other very special occasion?

This.

The inevitable breakup.

The bathroom door cracked open as she was belting her robe, and a very pretty—probably too pretty for her—man walked out. Naked. She picked up his clothes, turned them right side out, and handed them to him.

"This is me breaking up with you," Tammy said. "Not in the bathroom," she added when he opened his mouth to say something she didn't want him to say, didn't want to *hear* him say. "Not that we were together in the first place."

"We've been sleeping together for three months."

She lifted a brow. "We've been *fucking* together. That's it. That's what I made clear from the moment I brought you home from Bobby's."

"That's not—" His face crumpled and she allowed herself to feel like shit for a moment.

Just a moment.

Because she'd been clear with him.

But also like shit because clearly she'd fucked up, and he was hurting and that was on her. She wasn't a monster. She didn't like people feeling crappy, especially because of something she did.

Liking it or not, she still had to end this.

The longer it went on, the more he would expect her to give, and the more she would feel like she was kicking a puppy.

Good times.

Which was why she pulled her shroud of bitch around her.

"It's not?" she asked archly, yanking it tight, buttoning it up for good measure. They'd discussed this that first night, and again after, when it had been so good neither of them wanted just one time together. They'd talked about it many times over the last twelve weeks—that this was for mutual pleasure and not building a connection—never building a connection—and they'd usually done it when her instincts had prickled and told her that he might be feeling more than her.

She should have listened to her gut.

But he'd said all the right things, given her all the right reassurances.

And he was seriously talented at giving her orgasms.

But tonight had been different.

He'd made it clear they weren't just fuck buddies—or he didn't see *her* as a fuck buddy, while nothing about him had changed for her.

She wanted pleasure.

She wanted fun.

She didn't want a possessive, growly male who thought it was his right to claim her time and body—even if he was pretty.

"We've been together for three months—"

"Not together."

"We've..." He trailed off, probably realizing where he'd gone wrong.

"What?" she asked baldly, though not cruelly. She knew she needed to be firm in order for this to be a clean break. Clear boundaries. Not bending or giving in because that just made everything worse when it inevitably came down to this. "What?" she repeated when he didn't speak. "You thought you'd change my mind, even though I've made it clear I'm not interested in a relationship?" Catching herself fussing with the tie on her robe, she forced herself to stop, to not reveal this was uncomfortable, that she didn't like doing this. No cracks in her armor for him to slip back in. "We have fun together. I like your cock. I like *you*, but I don't want a boyfriend, and that's what you're trying to be. So, it's gotta be done, Adam."

"I—" He broke off again, and she pointed to the clothes. His shoulders straightened, and his expression went from hurt to mulish and—sigh, he was going to make this even harder. "You like me. We could be good together. I love—"

Panic washed over her, and quickly she shook her head, throwing her hand up, cutting him off with a sharp order. "Get dressed." Then she moved to the bedroom door, cloaking herself in sharp words before he got the rest of that statement out. "I'll clue you in," she said, zipping up the shroud of bitch jacket, pulling up her bitch pants, slipping her feet into bitch socks and shoes for good measure. "You're just upset because you're the one who usually ends things, add in that you're used to women fawning all over you because you're pretty." A beat. "And you are. You're gorgeous."

His face had changed from mulish to pained to gentle during her speech. When she called him gorgeous, that expression became determined.

Uh-oh.

"Just a little more time," he murmured, coming close and stroking his knuckles down her throat in the way that always made her shiver. He bent, trailed his lips along her jaw, and Tammy remembered why she'd brought him home in the first place.

And she almost gave in...

Almost.

Because the man had a cock that was...

"Please, love," he murmured. "I need—"

That snapped her out of it. He needed what she couldn't give him. What she wouldn't ever be able to give him. She couldn't be open in a way that would make him happy, and eventually, he would choose someone else.

It would be much less messy to end things now.

She gripped his shoulders, and though it was tempting to draw him near, to have one more time, she knew she couldn't.

Tammy shoved him back. "I'm done."

He reached for her again. "But—"

She shoved him away. Again. "*Done,*" she repeated, having done this too many times to do anything but end it here and now. Adam was a nice guy, and she'd kept him around for so long because he'd seemed on board to be a fuck buddy, but tonight...tonight he'd been different.

Tonight he'd made love to her.

Tonight hadn't been about mutual attraction.

He had feelings for her, and she couldn't let that stand. Better to cut ties now before he grew even more attached, before things got messier.

"Get dressed," she said again, exiting the bedroom and walking down the hall, moving to the front door.

It was better to be by an exit.

That made things less complicated...and easier to slam and lock the door.

A minute later, Adam emerged from the bedroom, shoving his cell and wallet into his pocket, his eyes blazing, but his expression gentle again. His lips parted as he lifted his arms, prepared to take her in his arms.

Fuck.

She sidestepped, gripped the doorknob, and opened the door.

"Bye, Adam," she murmured.

"Baby, come on," he pleaded, taking a step toward her. "We'd be good together."

"No," she said, stifling a sigh. This was seriously getting old fast. "We wouldn't."

"You like me."

She clenched her jaw. "Look, you're a nice guy, but—"

He came close, lowered his head, mouth closing in.

She put up her hand, pushed him back. "No."

"Tammy—"

"It's not you. It's me."

That finally seemed to penetrate, probably since it was such a shitty line, such a crappy thing to say. But at least it had the result of Adam backing away, his eyes furious. "Seriously?"

Tammy just lifted her brows.

He made a disgusted sound, but she was far too well-versed in this to feel guilty.

"Goodbye, Adam," she said.

A shake of his head, but he didn't say anything further, just walked down the steps.

She watched him get into his car, screech out of her driveway.

Sigh. Now she'd need to find a new source of orgasms. Rolling her shoulders, she started to turn to go back inside.

"It's not you, it's me?"

That voice was silk brushing along her thighs, dipping up to test the moisture between them. It was heat in her abdomen, fingers grazing her nipples. It was...instant sexual attraction, the same heady feeling she'd experienced the moment she'd laid eyes on Fletcher King. Eyes catching his as she'd strode to her office, desire pooling as she took in those blazing blue irises, his dark brown hair, so dark that it was nearly black. She'd clocked sexy stubble, a built body, and a great smile.

But he wanted *it.*

It being a real relationship, a girlfriend, a wife, and the picket fence. *It* being everything she couldn't give, because she wasn't a relationship, girlfriend, or wife and picket fence kind of woman. She'd heard him talk about *it* at work, heard the sadness in his words when he and his ex had broken things off.

She, on the other hand, wanted freedom.

More than she wanted the gorgeous man standing in front of her now.

"What are you doing here, Fletcher?"

"I need a favor."

The refusal was already on her lips. A favor that brought her sexy co-worker to her house on a weekend certainly didn't bode well for her.

But then he smiled, and she actually had to force her knees to lock so she didn't melt into a puddle, and...*that* right there illustrated just how much she didn't want to be in a relationship.

Because she'd been resisting this attraction with Fletch for an entire year.

Locking her knees, ignoring the melting, denying the temptation of him.

But that sexy smile, highlighted by the setting sun, the warm lights of her porch...undid her.

That sexy smile had her refusal staying lodged in her throat.

That smile had her saying...*yes.*

Eventually.

TWO

Fletcher

IT WAS four on Thursday afternoon.

He was half-convinced that Tammy wasn't going to show.

She'd been avoiding him all week at work like he was the plague, but when he'd stopped by her desk that morning—sneaking up on her so she couldn't snatch up her phone and pretend to make a call or haul ass to the bathroom in order to avoid him—she'd said she would meet him at his place so they could drive up to Tahoe together.

Well, she'd snapped at him that she'd made a promise and wouldn't go back on it.

So *said* was a loose description, and add in the fact that she was twenty minutes late, and he was starting to sweat it.

His mother was excited.

To meet his girlfriend.

The non-existent girlfriend he'd been pretending to have in the lead up to his younger brother's wedding. The one he'd been pretending to have because his family was worried about him after his breakup with Trina—and one had to say, the broken heart he'd ended up with. The one he began to pretend to have after he'd had a slew of almost girlfriends who'd nearly turned him off dating altogether, who made him wonder if his dream of making a family of his own that would be like the one he grew up with was something impossible.

Because he'd dated Roxy, who'd somehow managed to make a copy of his house key and then had moved her stuff into his place after three dates.

Then after he'd gotten the locks changed and her stuff back to her, he'd dated Lana. Lana had seemed normal for almost a month. Then when they'd first gone to bed together, she had declared her love...and when he hadn't been ready to express the same, she'd handcuffed him to her bed frame until he had.

Which he had.

Then he'd gotten the fuck out.

Those two should have clued him in that he was due for a time out.

But then he'd met Beth.

Gorgeous. Curvy. Pretty eyes. An ass...well, a *fantastic* ass.

She'd seemed perfect until he'd slept with her. And even the sex had been great. Explosive. Good chemistry. He'd given her an orgasm that had left her shaking...and then start crying.

Because she wasn't over her ex. And he wasn't her ex. And it felt wrong to have sex with someone who wasn't the person in her heart.

And since he knew what that felt like—to have his heart smashed with a hammer while trying to move forward, and not feeling right—he'd held her all night while she cried over her ex.

He'd willed away his erection—and one had to say his blue balls because even though Beth had gotten an orgasm, he hadn't —and wiped her tears.

Then he'd slipped out of her house and decided he was taking a break from women.

To refocus. To center himself. To not try and shove the puzzle pieces together when they didn't want to fit. Soon he'd look for someone to build a future with. Someone who wanted kids—one day. Who wanted to come home to him, and who he wanted to see at the end of the day. Someone he could have a relationship with that was like the one his parents had.

And maybe that sounded fucked up.

Because he should want his own thing, not replicate someone else, especially not his mom and dad's.

But, truthfully, his parents had it all.

Not easy. Not always smooth-sailing. They bickered over the proper way to load forks into the dishwasher, how to decorate their house, the Honey-Do list his mom loved to make. His dad's beater of a car that he was "fixing up" was a point of contention time and again.

But it was all based on love.

His dad always brought his mom a cup of coffee to bed in the morning.

His mom always made sure his dad's stash of Hot Tamales was in his desk drawer, even though no one was supposed to know about it.

They still went on dates and made out in the hot tub when they thought nobody was looking and recently, his dad had signed them up for ballroom dancing lessons because it was a dream of his mom's.

See?

Shit like that.

And Fletcher could go on for days with *shit like that.* Romantic, lovely shit that made him want something he wasn't sure he'd ever have. Especially with his track record of picking women who were—

A car pulled into his driveway, and he perked up when he saw the redhead behind the wheel.

She'd come.

He slumped in relief when she parked and climbed out of the car, her hair shining in the sunlight, her pale brown eyes glimmering like gemstones. She flounced over, the flowy sky-blue dress she was wearing billowing behind her.

"Tam—"

She continued her flouncing...right by him, walking straight for the passenger's side door of his car. "My purse is in the front seat, my bag in the trunk."

Then she got in.

And shut the door.

And...Fletcher stood there for a moment, staring at her, smelling the hint of her perfume—something that always reminded him of apple picking in the fall, floral and sweet—gaping because he'd never seen her in a dress.

She had nice legs.

Really nice legs.

So nice they were burned into his vision when he should be thinking of nothing more than getting through this weekend, playing a role, making sure that he didn't do something stupid and ruin their work relationship.

He loved his job at RoboTech.

Last thing he needed to do was create something toxic that affected his position just because he didn't want to be alone at his brother's wedding, couldn't bear the pitying looks tossed his way after Trina had broken things off with him at the rehearsal dinner. Only slightly worse would have been dumping his ass on the altar. Because she'd still done the dumping in front of everyone close to both of them. She just hadn't done it front of everyone close to them *and* two hundred other guests.

Fletcher sucked in a breath.

Get through the weekend.

Stage a breakup for this fake relationship at some future point.

Continue with his timeout from women.

Then reset and find something similar to what his parents had.

Easy enough.

Ha.

Unfreezing himself, he moved to her car, opened the door, and retrieved her purse, then walked around to the trunk and snagged the surprisingly large suitcase for three nights and days. It was fucking heavy, too.

Was she packing bricks?

Just to piss him off?

Maybe. He wouldn't put it past her, not when she'd practically made him crawl before she agreed to help him out—including letting her take over a project he'd busted to get for his department, lunch delivered to her desk for the next month, and coffee runs whenever she needed a fix.

It would have been a lot easier if they had more women in their department.

But their group was one of the few at RoboTech that had more men than women, and their department in particular had three women and nine men. One was his boss (off limits for obvious reasons). Another was seven months pregnant and happily married (and *that* would bring far too many questions, even if she did agree to accompany him). The last was Tammy, who was unequivocally beautiful, but she'd made it clear she had absolutely no interest in him.

As in, on her first day, he'd asked her to drinks—trying to be nice to welcome the new girl—and she'd shot him down with such force that he'd felt the sting for weeks.

But, look, he got it.

She hadn't known his intentions.

So, the next time inviting for post-work Happy Hours drinks was to be done, he'd made Barry—married happily to his partner of thirteen years—ask.

She'd accepted. They'd hung in groups. They'd worked together.

Peaceful friendship was eventually accomplished.

Now he might ruin it with a weekend of pretending to be dating. But he was desperate and willing to take that risk.

He just...wouldn't fuck it up.

Right.

Nothing would go wrong with *that*.

Somehow, he wasn't convinced.

THREE

Tammy

THE CAR SHOOK when he dropped her suitcase into the trunk.

And yes, it was heavy.

But this pretending she'd agreed to was for a *wedding*.

She needed heels—different pairs for the different outfits she'd brought—makeup, perfume, jewelry. Along with all the normal clothes and accoutrements she needed on a normal basis. Plus, it was cold in Tahoe this time of year. She needed a good jacket.

And snow boots.

Because what if it snowed?

They were going to the mountains. It snowed in the mountains.

Snow boots were heavy and took up room in a suitcase.

Hence the car shaking when it made its way into the trunk.

Her door opened, and Fletcher set her purse in her lap. Not in a huffy way that would have made her prickle and lash out, but gently into her lap, so she'd have it for the ride up.

Aw.

He was good guy.

She knew that—even though she was pushing him and being a bit of a jerk by flouncing around and making him lug her bags around. Still, because her work experience in the Bay Area had gotten off to such a rough start, she'd been guarded around Fletcher at first.

Guarded meaning surrounded in prickly rosebushes and hidden landmines prepped to blow.

Of one might say landmines were understandable given that her direct manager had done his level best to get her to sleep with him, even though she'd made it clear she wasn't interested. Multiple times.

Coalescing in her having to knee the asshole in the breakroom.

He'd dropped, moaned, and threatened assault.

Luckily, she'd had witnesses. She'd reported him to HR, gotten his ass fired, but because that process took so long and had been so painful—complete with him fighting it every step of the way and the department eventually divided over who was at fault (him, obviously)—she'd quit as soon as she had another position lined up.

Thankfully that new position was with some really great people at a very great company.

RoboTech was awesome.

Her work was awesome.

So, Fletcher asking her to drinks on her first day at the company had triggered her.

She'd thought that she'd ended up in the same situation she'd just left, and had panicked.

Eventually, though, she'd realized that the entire department went to drinks every Monday. His invite had been as a coworker wanting to include a new employee.

So...that had been a little awkward, given how brusquely she had shut him down. But once Tammy got over herself, she started going to Bobby's with everyone else, and she and Fletcher had built a good working relationship.

But now they were...fake dating?

And she was going to meet his parents...and potentially be in someone's wedding pictures?

Who's that girl in the corner of the dance floor?

Remember that bitchy redhead who mand Fletch carry all her things?

*Crop out Fletcher's (*cough* fake) ex from the family photos. She was so weird.*

Also—note to self—avoid the photographer like a son of a bitch.

Fletcher got into the car, glanced over at her, but didn't say anything as he pulled out of her driveway and navigated his way to the freeway. Silently. Which was the point that Tammy realized the silence would be continuing for the immediate time being.

And perhaps for the entire five-hour trip ahead of them.

Whatever.

Stifling a sigh, she got out her cell, plugged it into the dash, and blared her road trip playlist. No conversation? Might as well have music.

She was about ten bars into *Walk This Way* by Lady Gaga and really starting to groove when Fletcher unplugged her phone.

And pocketed it.

Pocketed *her* phone.

The music went off—obviously.

But...he put *her* phone in *his* pocket. And seriously, what the ever-loving flying monkeys was wrong with the man? Was she going to have to institute a tuck and roll on the freeway and abort this crazy plan?

Of course, the only reason that tucking and rolling might be survivable in the first place was because they were literally inching toward the Bay Bridge and its path that would lead up to the Sierras.

It's *path?*

Freeway? Hellish four lane road crammed with everyone trying to leave the city?

Both of those since she meant the highway clogged with cars leaving San Francisco, all trying to beat rush hour—and failing miserably.

Traffic wasn't the point, though.

"What are you doing?" she snapped, wanting to reach over and yank her cell out of his pocket, but since that would involve crawling practically onto his lap—since he'd put it in the pocket furthest from her—or at the very least put her hands next to a body part she'd been dutifully pretending he didn't have— Tammy found herself clenching her hands into fists and glaring at him.

"I spy with my little eye..." he began.

Her mouth dropped open. "Are you serious right now?"

"Something green," he finished.

"A tree." More snapping. "Now give me my fucking phone."

"Wrong," he said with sparkling blue eyes. Mischief and cool ocean waves. Damn the bastard, but that expression looked good on him.

She held her hand out, twitched her fingers. "Phone. *Now.*"

He just returned his gaze to the traffic.

And stayed silent.

Sigh.

Tammy turned her glare to the cars around them, inching forward on the approach to the lower deck of the Bay Bridge.

There weren't any trees around. Just cars and SUVs and trucks. Just buildings and billboards and the freeway itself. None of those were green. Except—

"That street sign," she said, pointing at the green rectangle with its rounded corners, white iridescent writing declaring the name of the street.

"Right," he said.

A blip of pride—stupid, she knew—but she still was satisfied to have gotten the answer right. Go her. She was killing it. This was what happened when she was one of four kids. Resources were scare, competition was high.

Victories even less frequent.

So, she'd take this one.

Even if it meant playing I Spy with a man who was gorgeous and had smiled his way into getting her to agree to fake date him.

With a man who still had her phone.

She extended her hand again, and gave him her patented angry eyes—the eyes that got men out of her house, the eyes that had always made her brothers quiver in fear. Unfortunately, her angry eyes didn't appear to have any influence on one Fletcher King.

He just glanced away from traffic, lifted a brow, and then turned back to stare out the windshield.

Silence descended.

They inched forward.

The silence grew heavier...along with her outstretched hand. So heavy, in fact, that she ended up dropping it to her lap with a sigh and returning her glare out the windshield.

"I spy..." he began.

"Oh, fuck you," she muttered, then exclaimed, "Ow!"

The fucker had flicked her in the ear, and damn, he must have practiced on his brother because that really hurt.

"Don't be an ass," he declared.

"*I'm* not the ass," she snapped. "That would be the person who took my fucking phone and won't give it back and—"

"It's rude to be on your phone. We're stuck in traffic with a long drive ahead of us. We should talk."

This man could *not* be serious. "Um...you're kidding, right?"

He lifted one shoulder in a shrug. Dropped it just as casually.

Fuck it. Here she went.

She was about to get up and personal with his lap and any potential snakes that might be (*were*) lurking beneath the cargos that were so lovingly encasing his thighs. Well, call her Steve Irwin because she was about to wrestle a croc. Unclicking her seat belt, she lurched across the console, shoved her hand into that pocket on the side of his leg, and yanked out her phone. He let her have it, but when she would have plugged it back into the cord, he pushed the button on the dashboard, turning off the radio completely, and then yanked that knob off, putting it in the same pocket that had held her phone.

The cord dropped to her thigh.

Her mouth dropped to what felt like the bay they'd just begun to drive over.

"I spy—" he started again.

And seriously *fuck* this. It was time for a tuck and roll. They couldn't be going more than a mile per hour. She'd be fine.

Tammy reached for the door handle.

Fletcher snagged her arm, circling her wrist, yanking it toward his lap. "What the fuck are you doing?"

"You're an asshole," she all but yelled, yanking her hand free. "We're going all of one mile per hour. I'm done. Thus, I'm getting the fuck out of here."

His mouth tipped up at the corners. "You realize I'm fucking with you, right?"

"You *realize* that I'm doing a favor *for you*, right?" she asked —okay, yelled. "And more than that, you spent the first twenty minutes of this drive ignoring me, and then the next taking away the source of my entertainment first in the form of music and then in the form of my phone. Could I have talked to you? Yeah. Am I obligated to entertain you like some circus animal? Especially when you're not willing to provide any entertainment yourself? No."

He winced.

"I didn't want to do this," she gritted out. "I *really* didn't want to do this. You laid out your case, and yes, I agreed in the end. But I'm not fucking doing *this*"—she pointed from herself to him—"for a whole weekend. I don't like people telling me what to do. I especially don't like it when *men* tell me what to do." She ground her teeth together. "Which is why I don't have, nor plan to *ever* have a fucking *boyfriend!*"

Silence.

Long, tense quiet that was so taut it seemed to fill the entire interior of the car.

Finally, Fletcher sighed and ran a hand over his face. "Fuck, Tammy. I *am* an asshole. I'm sorry."

Her brows lifted, but her angry eyes didn't fade. She didn't let them. "Yes, you are."

His gaze skated to hers then back out of the windshield. "I'm just...I'm in a weird mood."

She snorted.

Weird mood?

Fuck him.

Fuck him and his asshole tendencies. The next stop, she was getting a Lyft and getting the fuck home and—

"The next wedding I was supposed to go to was mine," he said softly.

Right. That sucked, but—

Tammy shrugged. "So, you steal my phone and try to strong arm me into playing I Spy because of that?"

Another wince. "As I said, I'm an asshole."

"And call *me* rude?"

Chagrin on that pretty face. "Yes, I believe I said I was an asshole." He sighed and shook his head. "I'm...not myself. Part because I'm not sure how to proceed with this, because you're doing me a huge favor and this whole thing could easily blow up in my face." He blew out a breath. "We're friends—kind of. But we're coworkers first, and I know your job is as important to you as mine is to me, and I don't want to fuck things up for either of us." His expression clouded and he thrust a hand through his hair. "And now because I'm a fucking coward, we're going to have to pretend to be dating and I asked you for a crazy big favor, *and* I'm already dreading the idea of lying to my family." His words finished on a whisper, and she felt some of her anger slid away.

"We don't have to do this," she said, patting his leg. "We can still go," she hurried to say when his face fell. "But we can just say we're friends. Or you can say I broke up with you and you have to go by yourself and—"

"I can't."

"Why?" she asked. Why was this so important to him?

Probably, she should have focused on finding out why pretending to be with someone had him not caring that she was extorting him for work, and instead just relieved that she'd agreed before she'd actually agreed to this charade.

A shake of his head.

"Why, Fletch?"

A muscle in his jaw twitched. "My mom—" A sigh. "She invited my ex-fiancé Trina, and Trina's new husband."

Ah.

Well, that explained part of it.

"So, you want to show Trina that you're not still hung up on her." *Even though it's clear you still are.*

That muscle ticked again. "Yeah."

"And you thought to accomplish this by playing I Spy?"

His fingers gripped the steering wheel tight. "We've established I'm an asshole. I got in my head. I panicked. I was trying to be a friend who kept his distance by doing stupid shit like taking your phone and playing I Spy rather than a man who's supposed to be dating you and liking you and enjoying your company because that felt wrong—"

"Ouch, jeez, you know how to treat a woman."

He cursed. "I didn't mean it like that." He sighed. "I'm taking advantage of you and I'm already feeling like an asshole for that. Then you played that song—"

Her brows drew together. "What's wrong with Gaga?"

A pause.

A long, long pause that had her wondering if he would answer.

"She played that song. Trina." He cleared his throat. "A lot."

Because it's fucking Gaga! And it's awesome. But Tammy didn't say that. Because she understood his reaction, got how painful those kinds of reminders could be. She didn't dwell on that, didn't add to that hurt. Instead, she just flicked *him* in the ear—and did it hard because she'd had three siblings to practice on—and said, "Next time just ask me to turn it off."

"Right," he muttered, rubbing his ear.

Ha.

Gotcha, bitch.

"And fuck I Spy," she went on. "I'm not nine years old."

"Got it." Another mutter. Another rub of his ear.

"And if I want to ignore you and look at TikTok on my phone for the next five hours," she said, "I'm going to do that."

A nod. "Understood."

"And—"

Humor had finally begun to enter his voice, the Fletcher she knew from work making a reappearance. "You're an independent woman who doesn't need my shit, is doing me a favor, and I need to get out of my own head and stop being an asshole otherwise you're bailing?"

Since that was basically the crux of the issue at hand, she just nodded.

He reached into his pocket, handed her the knob for the radio. "For what it's worth. I *am* sorry, and I'll curb the asshole."

"Good." She took the knob, shoved it back into place, and plugged in her phone again, cueing up her playlist. She played *Walk This Way* by Gaga because she was Tammy and fuck someone telling her what to do. But once the song was over, she switched to a rock and roll track that she assumed the nefarious Trina wouldn't listen to, and when that made him relax into the seat instead of clenching the steering wheel like it was a life preserver, she made sure to keep it on classics rather than her usually poppy sugary sweet songs.

Easy enough.

Her musical taste was eclectic.

Eventually the traffic cleared up, the sun started going down, and she turned down the radio. "Tell me about it," she said when he glanced over at her. "About Trina," she added when he just stared at her blankly.

"No." A cold rebuke.

"Yes," she pressed. "You told me that you needed a woman who wasn't going to get attached, someone who could take the pressure off your parents' matchmaking. You said I was the only one you knew who could help you." She nudged his arm. "You said I was in for a weekend of food, booze, and dancing. You *said* it wouldn't get complicated."

Yes, she was stupid to have believed that.

Yes, she'd already made it clear that she'd been made an idiot by his smile.

"This is getting complicated already," she pointed out. "And it's not about matchmaking, is it?"

"No." He went quiet. "And yes, I know, I'm making it complicated. I'm sorry for that. I know that's on me. I just didn't think I'd still be hung up on..." He trailed off and Tammy's cold, dead heart squeezed.

She felt bad for him.

She *shouldn't* be feeling bad for him. He'd been a jerk.

But she knew something of what it felt like to be on her back foot, to feel insecure and in a swirling maelstrom of thoughts, and to do the wrong thing.

"Pull over," she ordered.

His brows were raised when he glanced at her, but he shifted lanes and pulled off onto the shoulder.

"What—" he began.

She wrapped her hands around his head, yanked it toward hers. "Girlfriend practice time," she said, noting the shocked blue eyes.

For the record, shocked was an expression that looked good on him, too.

"Um—"

She kissed him.

FOUR

Fletcher

THE CAR WASN'T in park.

That was the first thing he thought when Tammy's lips hit his.

The next was—*holy fucking shit, the woman can kiss.*

Then the car rolled forward, and he slammed his foot on the brake, the gear shift into park, and turned, ready to haul Tammy over the console and into his lap. It would be a tight squeeze, but he'd make it work and—

She returned her tongue to her own mouth, dropped her hands, lifted her lips from his.

Patted his cheek.

Buckled her seat belt and sat casually on the leather, her fingers drumming on her thighs.

As though she hadn't just given him the best kiss of his life.

"What was that?" he rasped.

One shoulder lifted. "Girlfriend practice."

She'd said that once before, but it hadn't made any sense then, just like it didn't make sense now.

"Um, what?" he asked.

Not the most articulate of questions, but in fairness to him, all the blood had left his brain in favor of taking up residence in his cock.

Tammy was still as cool as a cucumber. "We couldn't have our first kiss be in front of Trina or your parents." A shrug. "I realized I should have thought of it sooner. We can't have a fake relationship if we've never even touched. We would look totally...well, totally *fake* and so"—she tilted her head from side to side—"girlfriend practice."

His lips were still tingling from the kiss.

His brain was hardly functioning.

That was the only explanation for why it took him so long to process her words.

Why he was still struggling to comprehend *girlfriend practice.*

But...Tammy made a fair point. Something he should have thought of well before he'd put this plan into place. His parents were observant. He and Tammy needed to come across as natural. Anything else and they'd know something was off. Plus, if he were being honest, he was game for girlfriend practice, especially if it involved Tammy's mouth on his.

Dangerous thought.

But it had been too long since he'd had sex.

"Fletch?" Tammy asked.

"Hmm?" He was distracted, thinking about how good the sex would be between them. Tammy had the typical complexion of a redhead—pale skin, freckles dotting her arms and face like a roadmap he wanted to trace with his tongue, especially the ones dancing over her cleavage.

Yeah.

He'd *love* to bury his face in her tits.

A pat on his cheek. "Focus, big guy."

He blinked, tore his gaze away from her breasts encased in the silky blue fabric he wanted to peel away, and met her pale brown eyes. "Right," he said.

"First step of that is driving." A nod toward the highway. "So, we can get this wedding over with while making Trina jealous as hell in the process."

"I'm an asshole," he muttered, shifting out of park and gaining some speed on the shoulder. Suddenly, he didn't care about making Trina jealous. He wanted to kiss Tammy again. He wanted to get to know her, to convince her to give him a chance.

"That's been established," she said dryly.

He snorted, checked traffic, and pulled back onto the highway, thankful that traffic had lightened up considerably. It helped that they were off the bridge and out of the major city centers. "Well, it's true. I've been all twisted up and acting like... I don't know. Not myself." Not the man he knew he could be. Not the man who'd get a chance with a woman like Tammy. "I promise I won't force you to play I Spy again."

"*Or* steal my phone?" she asked pointedly.

"*Or* steal your phone," he promised as he changed lanes. "*Or* the radio knob."

A flash of white teeth. Then she turned up the volume on a song that was popular on the charts right then. Not one he liked, but he wasn't going to comment. Now that he recognized his inner asshole, he was going to do his best to tell him to fuck off.

"Good," she said, settling back into her seat. "So back to girlfriend training. We need to cover the basics."

"Basics?"

"The things we need to know about each other," she said. Then added, probably in response to the confusion that was no doubt written on his face, "You know, the Big Eight?"

He shook his head.

"Oh boy," she said on a long-suffering sigh. "We're really having to start from scratch with this one, aren't we?"

He rolled his eyes but didn't comment.

"The *Big Eight*, my honeykins," she went on with mischief in her eyes, ticking off on her fingers as she listed, "Favorite meal, movie, cocktail, nonalcoholic drink, color, and flower—though the last is mostly for you to know about me. Then there are the either/ors. Beach or mountains. Coffee or tea. Night owl or early riser."

"That's nine."

"I believe I said that the flower one mostly applied to me," she said tartly.

"I can't have a favorite flower?" he teased. "Men can have favorite flowers, too."

A roll of her eyes. "Yes, Fletcher, of course, you can have a favorite flower. Okay, so the Big Nine. You start. And, since you've been waxing poetic about them, why don't you start by telling me your favorite flower?"

Shit. Now he needed to come up with a flower. What were those spiky, colorful ones his mom liked? All he could think was that Trina liked roses, so he hadn't bothered to pay attention to much else.

Pointy petals. Yellow. Dark middle.

Sunflowers!

Right. Those were the spiky ones his mom liked. He supposed those could be his favorite, too. They were cheerful, and he liked that they had other shades than just the traditional yellow—or at least the ones his mom usually had on her counter did.

"Sunflowers are my favorite," he said, "in case you were wondering what you should bring me on my anniversary."

His stare was on the road so he couldn't see her roll her eyes, but he felt it, and for some reason that made him smile. Mostly because he knew it wasn't real irritation she was feeling, and also because Tammy jokingly rolling her eyes at him felt normal. God knew she did it enough at work, at all of them. An exaggerated roll, the corners of her lips turning up, as though she were including them all in on the joke.

"There should be a Big Ten," he said.

A huff. "I don't care what your favorite bird is."

He snorted. "For the record, it's a penguin. They're always dressed to party and they waddle. How can you not love something that waddles?" he deadpanned, loving the soft laugh she gave him in return. "But in seriousness," he said when she fell quiet again, "the Big Ten needs to include you telling me about your family."

"Oh, Lord."

"What?"

"You're right." She tossed a smile his direction then affected a wince. "And you know how much I hate it when I have to say that."

God, how did this woman always made him feel better, feel lighter?

Because she was Tammy.

And Tammy was pretty fucking great—okay, no *pretty* about it. She was fucking great. No qualifications. Just a smart as hell, gorgeous woman who would put her weekend on hold to do him a favor, even though it was probably the last thing she wanted to do.

His heart squeezed, and suddenly proving to Trina, to his parents that he was over the breakup seemed much less important than winning over Tammy, than learning all the little things that made her tick.

Like the Big Ten.

Like hating to say he was right.

Fletcher chuckled. "That burn going down?"

"Like habanero salsa," she said dryly.

God, she was funny. Never missed a beat. Always was ready with a quip to lighten the mood. But more than that, he *liked* her. Sure, she'd been prickly to him at the beginning, but he'd understand why those spikes were in place after he'd overheard her telling Lisa, their boss, what had happened at her previous job.

She hadn't known they'd done Monday night drinks.

She hadn't known he was just trying to include her in the office bonding.

She'd thought he was trying to get in her pants, so had reacted in a way to keep him firmly at a distance.

And when she'd realized that Monday night drinks were a casual coworker get together, she'd joined in. Still careful about him, a firm barrier in place that he couldn't see but could feel, one that kept him proceeding on egg shells, trying to prove to her that he wasn't like the asshole from her old job.

He supposed the fact that she was in the car with him proved that he'd succeeded, at least in that respect.

Even though he'd shown up on her porch without warning, only having been there once before when he'd dropped her off after she'd drank a little too much one Monday night.

She would have been right to slam the door on his face, to go about her weekend—especially after the drama he'd stumbled upon. But she'd let him in, wrapped her tatty robe tighter around herself, and had gotten him a cup of coffee. Then had listened when he'd told her what he needed (okay, had begged her to be his date for the weekend).

Her face had been carefully blank. Her lips pressed flat.

It would have been easy for her to say no. Hell, he'd expected it.

But then she'd surprised him and agreed. Well...negotiated. *Then* had agreed.

"Your family?" he asked when she didn't say anything more about salsa, burning, or the Big Ten. "You have siblings, right? I feel like you've mentioned a brother." His gaze flicked to hers, and he was momentarily stunned by how beautiful she was with the sun going down behind them, its rays sliding through the rear window, turning her skin gold, bringing out the burnished highlights in her deep red hair.

Her smile was even more gorgeous.

Soft and full of love—so much love that he almost felt jealous that she was thinking about someone else (and not him—which had inner alarm bells blaring). He was jealous, and that was dangerous.

Friends.

Just *friends*.

Even if she kissed like a fucking goddess.

"I'm one of four," she said on a laugh. "The baby, and the one everyone loves the most"—a wicked smile that had him chuckling again—"And I have two brothers, actually. Jaime, the oldest, and Brad, and then one sister, Penny."

"Is Brad or Penny older?"

"Penny." A shrug. "For the record, the Huntington birth order is Jaime, Penny, Brad, and me." A laugh. "As I've established, the best of the Huntington brood. My parents are Andrew and Tawny, and they're awesome. Okay, your family. Go."

He went.

"Sean is my brother who's getting married, obviously. He's younger than me by five years. His fiancée is Carrie. They're a good match. Happy and have been together since high school. They were just both waiting to get married until they finished school and bought a house—the latter they managed last year."

Tammy whistled. "And they're what? Twenty-five, twenty-six?"

"Five. I just turned thirty." He gave her a rueful smile. "And I only managed to buy my townhouse last year."

"Me, too," she muttered. "The market is tough if you don't want to end up house poor. And I, for one, like to actually do things like go to the movies and on vacation." A shrug. "So, it took me a bit to save up, too."

Fletch nodded his agreement. "Well, if I didn't love Sean. I would hate him."

Curiosity filled her eyes when they met his for a brief moment. "Why?"

"His house is nicer."

She snorted. "Sounds like they had two people saving up. Bound to be nicer than what we managed to buy. But I know the feeling," she added when he made a face, "my siblings all have it together. They're married and in love, and the babies have begun arriving. Hell, my brother even has adopted a rooster, two cats, three dogs, and a trio of goats because his wife is an animal lover. Their house is like a fucking zoo—literally—but they love it."

"A rooster?"

"Sir Fuzzy McFeatherston."

"That's a mouthful."

She winked. "That's what she said." A grin paired with waggling brows that had him busting up and needing to concentrate so that he didn't swerve into the next lane. "But everyone just calls him the Fuzz for short. He walks on a leash, and wears a sweater vest. Hell, the Fuzz is almost as cute as the goats that wear pajamas."

For a second, he didn't think she was serious. But when she didn't laugh at the joke he thought she'd made, he felt his brows shoot up his forehead. "Goats that wear pajamas?"

"Yup. My sister-in-law is a nut." Another smile. "But I love her, and she makes my brother happy."

"And your other siblings, are they as happy?"

A nod. "Yup. That and more. In fact, their happiness is positively sickening." She nudged his arm. "And you? Obviously, Sean is happy since he's getting hitched. Is it just you two?"

"Just two boys," he said. "We had an older sister, but she died before I was old enough to remember."

"Oh, I'm sorry. That must have been hard for your parents."

"Yeah, it was. My mom still gets sad on her birthday every year."

She squeezed his arm. "I'm sorry," she said again.

He nodded.

"And you like Carrie for your brother?"

His eyes flicked to hers again, saw that she was looking at him gently. Sharp, fiery, didn't take any bullshit, but with empathy that was off the charts.

He'd seen it when Dawn—their pregnant coworker—had been so sick early in her pregnancy, and Tammy had brought her ginger candies and peppermint tea and the apple pear muffins from Molly's bakery that were the only thing Dawn could keep down.

He'd seen it with Lisa when her dog died, and Tammy had brought in a painting of him she'd had commissioned from Lisa's favorite picture of her and the pooch.

He'd seen it when she tried to pay for more than her fair share of Monday night drinks.

And he'd seen it with him, over coffee at her house after he'd randomly showed up on her porch, doing him a favor even though they weren't particularly close and what he was asking was a *big* fucking ask.

"Fletch?"

He blinked, pulled himself out of his head. "Carrie's great. My whole family is, actually."

"So, why the subterfuge?"

A nice way of asking why he was lying to his family about this.

A sigh. "I don't *like* lying to them. At all. We're close, and I just..." He cleared his throat. "My mom has been so worried about me since Trina, and I was in an okay place when she invited her—"

"I find that surprising," Tammy murmured.

"What?"

"Trina dumped you and hurt you deep enough that you don't want to be seen without some girlfriend armor." She shrugged. "It just seems strange that your mom invited her. Never mind that you would be okay with it."

"I pushed her to."

"Um..." She glanced at him, brows raised.

"What?"

"But why?"

It was his turn to shrug. "The moms were close. Really close." He paused, released a breath. "Truthfully, that's probably why Trina stuck with me for so long. Our moms are best friends, have been almost from the moment we started dating. Our families were so close, and...well, it took her a bit to tell me she wasn't happy. Like more than a bit."

"What does that mean?"

"It means...she told me at the rehearsal dinner it wasn't going to work."

Tammy winced.

"I know," he admitted. "I was blindsided at first. Now, I understand it more. There were things I ignored..."

He sighed.

Yeah, it had felt like shit after the wedding was called off. Not just because he'd had a broken heart and because he'd been embarrassed how it all went down, but it hurt more to lose part of his family, for his brother and parents to be feeling the same loss of Trina and her family as deeply as he had fucking. "At first everyone stayed separate, and things were really tense. But it was hurting my mom to stay apart from Trina's mom. So, I pushed and made sure the invite didn't get lost in the mail."

Tammy's question was quiet. "Why?"

"Like I said, I was in a good place," he said. "So, it wasn't all noble. I was happy, had put the breakup behind me, and was ready to start dating again, so I thought there wasn't a need for everyone to be separate." He gripped the steering wheel. "I made my mom arrange a dinner with both families, and I made it clear that I didn't want to be the reason we couldn't be close again. Trina came, we talked a lot of it out, and she agreed with me about wanting our families to stay connected. Everyone eventually got over it, and because Sean's wedding date was set, I made sure he invited Trina and her parents."

Tammy made a noise.

Surprise? Shock. He didn't know.

She asked, "Then what happened?" before he could ask her to explain.

"They agreed to come to the wedding—all of them—and Carrie didn't dismember me for daring to invite people to her big day. We had pie." He made sure his voice was even. "With ice cream." A breath. "Then Trina shared that she was married. Had eloped with the guy she'd been dating."

Shocked silence. Then, "Oh, shit."

He sighed. "Exactly. I wanted to be happy for her," he whispered. "We'd been together too long for me to not want her to be happy."

Tammy's voice was gentle. "But she was married."

"After six weeks and a handful of dates."

"Jesus."

"Yeah."

"So that's why you went warp speed with the dating."

Not a question. It still made him frown. But he gave her the truth anyway. "I definitely jumped in hard and heavy."

"And it must have been *so* hard for all those women to fall in love with you," she said dryly.

"What are you talking about?"

She fiddled with the radio. "I know about the girls. Hell, the other guys in the office can't stop talking about how hot they are, and how many of them you keep getting."

Wow.

If she only knew.

"Let me tell you," he muttered, "no amount of attractiveness could make me go on another date." A beat. "With *any* of them."

"That bad? Worse than going to a wedding alone?"

"Worse than giving up the Carter project," he said, naming the task she'd negotiated for. The project was a cool one, charting and exploring hirings, promotions, and managers— from department heads all the way up to the executive level. RoboTech was a women-owned company, and they were probably more diverse than most of the Silicon Valley and San Francisco based tech businesses. But their CEO, Heather O'Keith had never been satisfied with probablies. She wanted data. And progress. Basically, this was the type of project that would get someone noticed by the important higher ups.

Which was why it had stung to let it go.

Not as much as the pity that would be in his family's eyes, though, if he showed up to the wedding single and miserable and...

Could he get a side of pathetic?

Everyone was happily paired off.

Except him.

And the only reason he wasn't driving up alone was because he'd bribed a woman to spend the weekend with him.

Cool.

"I'm scared to ask," she said.

"Let's just say that the six weeks Trina took to elope would have been too long for them."

"Yikes."

"Yeah."

"So now you've got me," she murmured.

Said quietly, with a hint of some underlying emotion that he couldn't tease free of the words. He glanced at her, skin still golden in the fading sunlight, her features delicate and beautiful. She was smart and kind and fierce, and a man would be lucky to have her.

Which was why he reached over the console and brushed a thumb over her jaw.

She turned, met his eyes.

"Why?"

A blink, confusion trickling into the pale brown of her irises. "Why what?"

"Why did you say it like that, sweetheart?"

FIVE

Tammy

WHY DID you say it like that, sweetheart?

"Say what?"

But she had the feeling she knew what she'd accidentally let bleed into her voice. Something she didn't think about. Something vulnerable and throbbing and painful that she'd locked up long ago.

"You said, '*So now you've got me.*'" His thumb brushed over her skin once more, so light that she barely felt it. "Why did you say it like you're some bad carnival prize?"

Um.

"Fletcher," she said. "You know who you're talking to, right?"

He lifted his brow.

"You don't need to be soft with me. Don't need to think I'm one of those women saying one thing when I really want another." She'd been cured of *that* notion long ago, of wanting anything *more*. "I'm chronically single because I choose to be. I don't have the mental bandwidth to be a good girlfriend without bribery. That guy from last weekend—"

"The *it's not you it's me* guy?"

She winced then nodded. "Yeah. Him. We were fuck buddies for three months. He wanted more. I didn't. I cut it off." A swirl of guilt despite telling herself that she had nothing to feel bad about. He'd known where she stood. "I broke up with him via text."

Fletcher glanced at her, concern on his face. "And he came over to your house—"

"No," he explained. "I broke up with him by text while he was *at my house*. In the bathroom. Because he..."

Fletcher frowned. "Because he what?"

Ugh. She didn't want to talk about this. But the pain in her ass had opened up to her, had laid it out there, and she found she couldn't leave him hanging without giving at least a little. "Because he made love to me."

A pause. "You *did* say you were fuck buddies, right?"

"Yeah."

"So..." He trailed off, paused. "I'm failing to understand the problem, sweetheart."

The second time he'd called her that. Twice more than she normally would allow, but because they were supposed to be dating and *in love*—blegh—she let it slide. "We were fuck buddies. No feelings. No *love* allowed. It was about mutual orgasms and nothing more, and...he forgot that."

"Wow."

Fletcher's tone said he wasn't impressed.

"What?" she snapped, defensive now. "Men do this shit to women all the time, and no one gets on their asses for remaining unattached. Just because I'm a woman—"

"It's not that."

She waited.

When he didn't answer, she said, "So a man gets a high five for fucking around, but I get derision just because I want the same."

"No, Tam." He glanced at her. "It's just that I think it's hard for feelings to stay separated when you're sharing your body with someone."

"Which is why I don't normally do repeats," she said. "Adam, however, convinced me to take that chance. Then convinced himself I would change my mind." She snorted. "Like he could fuck me into becoming the adorable little wifey. I want a career. I like my house and my mattress. I paid a fucking *ton* for my pillows and sheets. I'm happy with the world I've built for myself, and I don't need a man in it."

She had herself.

Her family.

Her friends.

She never felt like anything was lacking. Not anymore, anyway.

"Of course, you don't," he said.

"So, don't give me a lecture on how *women* can't keep their hearts separate of their body," she snapped. "I'm perfectly happy doing things my way."

"I'm happy you're happy." He signaled, changed lanes, and passed a slow-moving truck. "But *I* definitely couldn't hack it. I've slept with four women, and I found it difficult to separate my feelings from them, even *when* it was time to end things— case in point, me getting dumped at the rehearsal dinner."

"And the others?" she found herself asking.

"Another case in point, because I struggled to break up with them, even when it was unhealthy."

"*How* was it unhealthy?"

He told her about the trio of women who'd prompted him to take a dating break.

"*Handcuffed* you?" she exclaimed once he'd told her about Lana.

He nodded grimly.

"And the other one copied your *key?*" she exclaimed. "Without asking you?"

Fletcher shook his head. "Yup." A beat. "And she made *two* copies, which I found out after I'd ended things and came home from work to find her naked in my bed."

"Wow."

"Yeah."

They drove in silence for a bit. "And I thought the moving in some clothes was bad."

"Now you know why I'm off women."

That was a sad thing.

Because despite the bumpy start of their drive, Fletcher was a good guy. Always on time, always pulled his weight, always paid for his share when the office went out for drinks or tapas. He didn't letch on her if she wore a low-cut blouse. His gaze was always kept firmly on her face. He was funny, and she liked that he cared enough about his family to patch things up with his ex.

She'd had no shortage of good (albeit imperfect like all other humans) male role models in her life, so it was easy to know where he fit in.

Occasional douchery.

Mostly good.

She needed to figure out who to set him up with. Of course, not herself, and with only Cora single in their group of friends, it wasn't like she had a ton of resources when it came to singles who were ready to mingle. But—

"Do you date Black women?"

His eyes flicked to hers, a smile on his handsome face. "I date *all* women. Tall, short. Skinny, plump. I love them all."

Good.

She held up her phone, snapped a picture, the flash bright in the dim interior of the car.

He rubbed his eyes before turning back to the road. "What are you doing?"

"Setting you up with my friend, Cora," she said, typing out a message. "She's hot, curvy, has great hair, and is smart as hell. She's"—chef's kiss—"absolute perfection. And she's single and not going to move herself into your house after two dates."

"It was three," he muttered.

"Semantics. And"—she tapped at the screen—"sent. That sexy smile of yours will definitely catch Cora's eye."

"You do realize it's weird that you're setting me up while pretending to be my serious girlfriend, right?"

"Is it giving you thruple vibes?"

"What's a thruple?" he asked, a deep vee between his brows.

Amusement bubbled up in her, and she rubbed her hands together, evil genius style. "Oh, you sweet, innocent thing. Let Auntie Tammy educate you. A thruple is just a relationship with three people."

He rolled his eyes. "That sounds like drama waiting to happen. I could barely handle one woman."

"It's not like that. It's...when three people are mutually in a relationship. Not like you're trying to juggle two women at once."

"Still too much work for me."

She giggled. "And definitely too much for me, so I can't give you too much shit. Hell, I don't want one person, let alone two."

"Why don't you want it anyway?"

"Want what?" she asked, playing dumb.

"A person. *Your* person." Her heart—the damned misbehaving thing—squeezed at the soft way he said that. "The one who'll have your back, who you're excited to go home to every night."

A memory flashed and was trailed by a painful pulse slicing through her insides that had her forcing out a breath to keep her voice even. "I think we established that already," she said lightly. "I like sex. I don't like being tied down. No relationship necessary."

Not ever again.

Deep blue eyes on hers, studying her closely.

Tammy held her breath, kept her expression neutral.

He turned back to the road. "Right, so why don't you educate me on the Big Ten then. I know about your family, so I need the rest."

Thankful for the change in topic, she began ticking off items on her fingers. "Favorite meal—meatloaf and mashed potatoes."

"What? Really?"

She grinned. "I grew up in the Midwest, baby. Nothing more that I love than a meal that can stick to my ribs." He chuckled and she liked that, liked making him laugh. "What's yours?"

"Meatloaf and mashed potatoes," he quipped.

Tammy rolled her eyes. "What's it really?"

"My mom makes homemade pasta, simple flavors—Parmesan, pepper, and the noodles themselves. It should be boring." He shrugged. "But it's delicious, and I always beg my mom to make it for me when I visit."

"If she's anything like my mom, I bet she loves that."

She watched the half of his mouth she could see curve up, and seriously, did the man have to have such a gorgeous smile? It threatened to melt her brain—*had* melted her brain to get her to agree to this scheme. "That she does." A beat. "Though she loves to moan the whole time she's making the dough about how hard it is." His head turned toward hers, the other half of his mouth joining the first in turning up. "That way I feel guilty and knead it for her while she's telling me all the ways I'm doing it wrong."

Laughter bubbled up in her throat. "Now *that* also sounds like my mom. She's wonderful, of course, but she has a vested interest in doing things *her* way."

"Because it's the best way, obvs."

She snorted. "Obvs?"

A smirk. "It's what all the cool kids are saying."

Now her humor didn't just stay in the back of her throat. It danced over her tongue, slid through her lips. He joined in, his rough chuckles intertwining in the air with hers. She really liked that sound, liked that they could joke and laugh. It was nice. It was like what she had with Cora and Kate, Heidi, Kels, and Stef.

Friends.

She may not be down for searching for a soul mate.

But she was always down for more friends.

Next, he quizzed her on her favorite cocktail—rum and coke, *obvs*, because the classics were sometimes best. He liked a beer from a local brewery—apricot-flavored. That wasn't a cocktail, but she let it slide, especially when he told her that his favorite movie was *Die Hard*, because that was hers as well, and if she'd still believed in soul mates, she'd be all over believing that this man was hers. Because both of their favorite colors were blue, and she loved sunflowers like him, and they each preferred the beach and coffee to tea and mountains.

Pretty much the only thing they *didn't* agree on—aside from the fact that he wanted the white picket fence and woman in a big poofy dress—was that he was an early bird, and she was a night owl.

But she knew that already.

He was usually the first one to yawn and pull up stakes at

Monday night drinks, the first one in the office in the morning, making sure the coffee pot was full of the steaming black lifeblood for those who stumbled in later.

For *her* who stumbled in later.

They bickered a bit about the merits of sleeping in versus getting up and at 'em early, and then they began bickering about sports—she was a hockey fan, he preferred baseball (barf). Eventually they started discussing birthdays—hers September 8th, his October 9th—their favorite pastries from Molly's—chocolate croissants for her, the mocha chocolate cupcakes for him, the delicious fried food smorgasbord from Bobby's, and the plans for the weekend.

Cocktails and some food tonight with his family.

A morning hike and a late lunch with the fam tomorrow morning, followed by the rehearsal in the evening, dinner afterward at a restaurant right on the lake.

Saturday. Pre-wedding breakfast.

Then Fletch would go off to do best man duties, and she'd be on her own until wedding time.

Ceremony. Reception. Cake and bouquet tosses. Dancing.

And Sunday they'd have breakfast with his parents then GTFO, getting back to reality and being coworkers, and she'd get her hands on the Carter project.

"My mom can be a little much," he was saying as they wound their way up through the highway twisting through the mountain pass. "So, if I'm gone and it gets to be too much for you just text me and I'll—"

Another one of those strange pulses slid through her. "It won't be too much."

His fingers tightened on the steering wheel. "Well, if it—"

"It won't." She dropped a hand onto his thigh. "I'm good with parents. I'm *so* good, in fact, that I've got an advanced degree in pushy moms." A squeeze. "I can handle myself. You just do what you need for your brother to make his day great, and in the meantime, we'll convince everyone you're blissfully happy and get everyone off your back. Okay?"

Now his knuckles were white. "But—"

"No buts." Another squeeze. "I may not want a boyfriend in reality, but you've paid me handsomely, so I'm going to be the best fake girlfriend around."

She laughed.

And after a beat that lasted long enough for her to glance up at Fletcher's pretty face, he joined in. Then he squeezed her fingers, peeled her hand from his thigh, and set it gently into her lap. He was smiling at her, the bright, gorgeous smile, as he said, "Damn right, you are."

She couldn't help and think she'd just missed something.

But then he was talking again, and the smile was there, and they were driving down the road to his parents' place, and there wasn't time to ponder what she'd missed.

Because it was time to put her advanced degree in pushy moms to good use.

SIX

Fletcher

TAMMY WAS GOOD.

Really good.

His mom—as one's mom did—practically ran out onto the porch the moment she heard his car pull into the driveway, barely waiting for him to put the transmission into park before she was tugging open his door and hugging him tight.

By the time she released him, Tammy was out of her door, her purse on her shoulder, and walking around the front of his car.

His mom released him and straightened, beaming when she saw Tammy standing near the hood. "Hi, Mrs. King," Tammy said, moving toward them and extending her arms. "I'm Tammy. It's so nice to finally meet you."

And then she was hugging his mom.

"Connie, please," his mom said, squeezing her back. "I'm so glad you're here."

Tammy pulled back. "Thank you for letting me crash the

wedding. I know it's got to be inconvenient, being so last minute and all."

Fletcher winced. He'd asked Tammy last minute, but he'd accepted the invitation on her behalf months ago.

"Last minute?" his mom asked. "But—"

Tammy's gaze flickered, going from his to his mom's and she knew she caught the error. Her recovery was swift and much faster than his would have been. "I know weddings are planned in months to years," she said quickly. "So, I'm honored to be included." She shifted slightly, reached into her purse. "I brought this for you." Her hand emerged, a small, wrapped package in her hands.

And his mom looked like she'd achieved nirvana.

"For me?"

Tammy nodded. "It's just a little something to say thank you for having me."

His mom opened the package—she was a present lover and her lack of patience was well-known in his family—revealing some sort of lotion that made his mom squeal. "I love this brand!"

Tammy smiled. "I'm glad."

"Aw, honey, you're so sweet. Come on"—she laced her arm with Tammy's—"let's get you inside. Did you eat? I have left-over lasagna if you're hungry."

"Lasagna sounds awesome if it's not too much trouble."

"It's not," his mom said. "Do you like lemon drops?"

A flash of white. "I do."

"Food. Drinks." She drew Tammy toward the house as she tossed over her shoulder, "I'll send your dad out to help with your guys' bags, honey."

"I've got it," he called as the pair reached the front door. "Though I may break my back with how heavy Tammy's bag is."

Tammy shot him a glare, but her voice was sickly sweet when she said, "Thank you, baby."

"No problem, sweetkins."

The glare softened, amusement gentling her features.

Then she went inside, his mom at her side, leaving him to haul in her suitcase—which, as he hefted it up onto the porch, he was convinced was full of bricks—into the house. He dragged it through the front door, dropping his backpack next to it.

His tux was already up here, fitted during one of the many visits he'd made over the last few months, so other than a couple of changes of clothes, he didn't need much.

Just his fake girlfriend he'd paid for handsomely.

His insides knotted themselves up tight, and he felt sick.

When things with Lana had been going well—before the handcuffing and forcing him to declare his love (and then the calling of the police and the getting a restraining order)—he'd thought he would have someone awesome to bring to the wedding.

Then, when things had soured, he'd thought Beth was the one he'd bring.

That obviously hadn't worked out.

So, two months ago, with no prospects on the line and a trio of short relationships that had told him he needed a break from women and dating, he'd intended to just go solo. Then he'd come up for a visit and had overheard his mom gushing to Trina's mom. Saying she was glad he and Trina were both paired off and happy because she'd hated seeing him so miserable.

She didn't know about Roxy or Lana or Beth.

Because he hadn't shared the handcuffs and house keys and holding her while she sobbed because he wasn't the man she loved. Instead, his mom only knew that he was dating someone, and it was going well.

And miraculously, his mom had never asked her name.

Not until a week ago.

It had always just been *his girlfriend* or *his woman*. He could only thank the stress of planning the wedding—Carrie's parents were gone so his own parents were doing double duty, and his mom was playing the mother of both the bride and groom. Dress shopping, interviewing photographers, DJs, florists. She'd eaten it up, helping Carrie plan a wedding she'd never thought to have after having lost his sister.

So, the distraction of the wedding meant that he'd been off the hook.

At least until they were making place cards last weekend and realized they hadn't known his nonexistent girlfriend's name.

Pressed, he'd said the one person he could think of who wasn't his boss or pregnant.

Tammy.

Who was beautiful and apparently good at charming parents because both his mom and dad hadn't worn smiles like that since Sean had announced he and Carrie were getting married.

Tammy was talking animatedly, a martini glass in her hand.

"Your house is lovely, and these counters"—she ran her free hand over the polished surface—"they're absolutely gorgeous. Are they granite?"

"Quartz," his dad said, his chest puffing out.

Probably because even though his parents were best friends and kept the love alive in a number of ways, they couldn't agree over any decor for the house—from kitchen counters to Christmas lights. Their biggest fights had always been over paint colors and picture placement.

And those counters had been one of the biggest fights of all.

Ending with his dad ordering them without his mom's

involvement.

Timing their arrival and installation so that it happened when Fletcher's mom was off for a girl's weekend. She'd come home to a kitchen that was finally completely upgraded...and she'd been absolutely furious with his dad's underhandedness.

She'd threatened the guest bedroom.

But as always, they'd made up before going to sleep, and all had been good...until his mom had the cabinets repainted while his dad was away on a fishing trip.

For his part, he liked the color his mom had picked *and* the quartz his dad had chosen.

Not that he'd commit to either of those sentiments, since it was the surest way to get his parents' hackles up. Just like he could see his mom's lifting at the compliment that Tammy had given.

Fuck, he'd need to wade in and—

"And those cabinets," Tammy went on. "The color is to *die* for." She got up and brushed her fingers over one of the doors. "I love how it's the perfect mix of blue and gray. And these knobs" —crystal pulls Fletch's dad *hated*—"Tony," she said turning to Fletcher's dad. "I think it's so cool that you have these in the house. I always say that real men love glitter, isn't that right, baby?"

It took him a moment to realize that she was roping him into the conversation.

Dangerous.

But mostly because he really liked the way that she called him *baby*.

"Yeah," he agreed when she stared at him, deliberately lifting her brows. "Glitter is life."

She snorted softly but didn't move when he slid an arm around her shoulders and stepped close. He told himself that it was to keep up the I, but he wasn't sure it was *only* that. Which was a train of thought he wasn't going to focus on. Push it down, pretend that this was all fine and light and this was perfectly normal to be talking about glitter with his parents and fake girlfriend.

His dad laughed, shook his head. "I see you got a good one there," he said and wound an arm around his mom's waist, tugging her close and kissing her hard and long and far too deeply in front of other people.

But these were his parents.

They'd never been shy about showing their emotions—whether they were angry or amorous. He was used to it, and he wondered if Tammy's parents were like that too, because she just sipped her drink and continued admiring the cabinets and those crystal pulls.

"Are your parents like them?" he found himself asking, needing to know the answer, the gnawing urge to know *everything* about her intense. When her gaze met his, he nodded at his mom and dad still kissing on the other side of the island.

She lifted a brow. "How do you think I got my advanced degree in girlfriend etiquette?"

He chuckled.

She grinned.

A lock of hair slid forward over her cheek, and he brushed it back, tucking it behind her ear. Couldn't help letting his fingers drift down her throat following the long, silken strand as it curled against her pale skin.

Her lips parted, her breath shuddering out.

He leaned close, let his fingers drift lower. Over one collarbone, the other, then tracing the neckline where it hugged the upper curves of her breasts. Inappropriate. Not contact they'd agreed upon. But Tammy drifted closer, stared up at him with heat in her gaze, and he found himself tracing the line of that fabric again and then again—back and forth, back and forth.

Rough lace.

Silken skin.

A flush growing on those tempting globes, spreading across her chest, beneath the neckline of her dress.

He wanted to peel the fabric away, to see how far it had spread.

To kiss every inch of her skin.

Except...

Paid handsomely.

Right.

Fake. This was all fake.

Luckily, Tammy's stomach growled. Loudly. Loudly enough that his parents broke apart—well, his mom pulled back, declaring, "You're hungry! Let me feed you," as she pushed out of his dad's arms and bustled to the fridge, pulling out a couple of containers. "Sit. *Sit!*" She gestured at the stools. "Tammy, do you need another drink? Tony, get her a refill, and get your son a beer."

Drinks were doled out.

Lasagna was reheated, along with some bread.

Salad was plunked onto plates; forks were passed across the table.

And all the while, his mom beamed and puttered around, looking happier than he'd seen her in ages.

Because Tammy was great and charming and proving she had that advanced degree in wooing parents, so his mom didn't have to worry about him anymore. And his brother was getting married in two days to a woman they all loved.

Their lives were all neatly packaged.

Her boys were happily paired off.

Everything was good.

Except it was all a lie.

SEVEN

Tammy

HE'D GOTTEN quiet at dinner.

She'd thought it was because she and his mom were dominating the conversation, or maybe that he was worried she'd be upset he'd all but caressed her breasts while his parents were sucking face.

She should be.

But truthfully, all she'd been thinking about was how good it had felt to have him touching her.

If he wasn't looking for picket fences and engagement rings, Tammy would have been all over that, though preferably without the side of parental supervision.

Grinning, she went into the bathroom and washed her face, scrubbing off the day's makeup and slathering on her moisturizer. His parents were as bad as hers were with the PDA, but it was nice that they so obviously still loved each other. It made for a much less complicated weekend than if she had to weave her way through a mom and dad who loathed one another.

Done with her face, she brushed and flossed and mouth-washed—the lasagna was delicious, but Connie wasn't one to skimp on garlic—then quickly combed and braided her hair. Pajamas were next, and only a few minutes later she was back in the bedroom.

With Fletcher.

Who was wearing a pair of basketball shorts.

And nothing else.

And—ho, mama—she was thanking the gods of masturbation because the man was *hot*. Long and lean, pecs that she wanted to grab, biceps that would be easy to hold on to when he lifted her up and fucked her against the wall, or when he was on top of her and was pounding into her, or when—

She tore her gaze away and moved to the side of the bed he hadn't claimed, spending a couple of moments plugging in her phone and setting her hand cream on the nightstand before climbing under the covers and beginning to rub the lotion onto her skin. "Bathroom is all yours," she murmured, chancing a glance at him from beneath her lashes. He hadn't moved, was still standing there in those basketball shorts that were riding low, making it so damned tempting to...just...push... them...down.

Tammy would bet the Carter project that the man was built.

Mostly because she could see the man was *built* through the thin material lovingly cupping—

She choked.

On her own drool.

But at least the sound broke her focus, and drew Fletcher back into his, it seemed. He turned and headed into the bathroom, the door *clicking* closed behind him.

She released a breath she hadn't known she'd been holding and finished with her hand cream, sliding down onto the mattress, and tugging the covers up to her chin. Sleep coming up to swallow her down would be really good right about now, because her inner devil was urging her to follow him into the bathroom, to nudge down those shorts, and—

A knock at the door.

Not the one leading to the bathroom.

She started to toss back the covers, but before she got more than a hand on the edge of them, the door opened, and Connie poked her head in. Her eyes were closed. "I'm not looking, honey. I just forgot to bring you the extra blankets for the bed."

Tammy bit back a smile and slid out from the comforter, glad her PJs kept her well covered up. "It's okay, Connie. I'm decent." She moved to the door as Connie opened her eyes, scanning the space. "Fletch is in the bathroom," she said, taking the blankets. "Thanks for these. I'm guessing it gets pretty cold at night?"

A nod.

Then fingers brushed the arm of her pajamas. "I'm sorry," Connie murmured. "They just look so soft. And they *are*," she breathed. "Wow."

This was a woman after her own heart.

Knew her mind, loved garlic, and appreciated a good pair of pajamas.

With that, Tammy made a decision.

She set the blankets on the edge of the bed and went to her open suitcase, propped on a small loveseat along one wall, rustling in it, and pulling out what she was looking for. "Here," she said, bringing out the set of new pajamas, their tags still on because she'd picked them up just that morning. "You're my size, and these are brand new. Try them tonight. They're yours if you like them."

"Oh, I couldn't—"

"*Could*," Tammy said. "My mom got me hooked on these. Let me share the wealth, okay?"

"I—"

The bathroom door opened, and Fletcher strode out, still in the sexy as hell shorts, still topless and gorgeous and...lickable.

He skittered to a stop. "Mom!"

Tammy managed to tear her eyes off the flat abdomen she wanted to kiss her way down and move her gaze to his face.

His *outraged* face.

"Your mom was just bringing extra blankets," Tammy hurried to share. "My blood fails when it comes to keeping this city girl warm in the mountains." Never mind that she'd grown up with winters and snow and temperatures probably lower than they'd get here. One, she was spoiled already with her California weather. Two, Fletcher looked very close to losing his temper. He was a pretty even-keeled guy, but his mom barging in on him and his "girlfriend"—yes, with quotes—certainly wasn't making him happy. "Thanks again, Connie," she said, "and let me know how you like the PJs, okay?"

Connie sputtered. "I—I—"

"Goodnight, Mom," Fletcher gritted out.

Connie recovered and kissed Tammy on the cheek. "Night, honey. Night, baby," she called to Fletcher.

Then she was gone.

Fletcher strode to the door, flicked the lock. Then sighed and shook his head. "Pointless. She's probably learned lock-picking skills somewhere along the way."

"Want to shove a chair in front of it?" Tammy said lightly.

He scowled at her, seemed to be considering dumping her suitcase on the floor and the size of that loveseat, before sighing and rounding the bed. "You still good with us sharing?" He nodded at the blankets bundled on the edge of the mattress. "I can bunk on the couch."

Probably, it would be smarter for him to do that.

But her toes were already chilly, and it was going to only get colder. Plus, if he was right about his mom's lock-picking skills then it would be odd for him to be sleeping on the couch.

She nodded. "I'm good with sharing. So long as you're not a blanket hog."

His lips tipped up. "I'm a very reasonable blanket sharer."

"All right then." She crawled back into bed, brought the covers up again, and deliberately closed her eyes. If she could just pretend this was normal, she would fall asleep, and everything would be good and—

The bed rocked.

The covers shifted.

Heat pooled between her thighs.

Needy. She was so *damned* needy.

But...picket fences and pretending. So, she closed her eyes and concentrated on breathing, on ignoring that Fletcher was also breathing next to her (funny how that happened), on ignoring the slight bounce when he reached up to turn out the lights.

And also the quiet rustle of him getting settled.

The faint gleam of the moonlight projecting the shadows of his movements on the wall in front of her.

The...

Finally—thank God, *finally*—sleep came up and yanked her under.

He'd lied.

He *was* a blanket thief.

Even when she'd woken in the middle of the night and pulled the blankets from the foot of the bed over her, she'd been awakened barely an hour later, ass in the cold, her body wracked with shivers.

There'd been a battle—her trying to yank some blanket free, him dead to the world and shoving it beneath him—and she'd lost, moving as close as she dared to him, shivering as sleep took her under again.

Then had woken barely an hour after that, with *her* beneath him, his arms wrapped tight.

She should move.

But he was warm, and his grip was tight, and she knew that it was pointless to try to escape.

She hadn't even managed to secure a corner of the blankets. With his arms around her, holding her flush against him, she wouldn't make it more than a few inches.

And truthfully, he was warm, and she didn't *want* to escape.

So, she just let her eyes slide closed, snuggled up to his warmth, and fell asleep in Fletcher's arms.

Dangerous.

And yet, she couldn't bring herself to care.

EIGHT

Fletcher

FLOWERS AND FALL in his nose.

Soft curves beneath his palms.

Sighing, he shifted, hips arching forward, his cock coming in contact with a generous ass. A moan in his ears. A hand drifting up to weave into his hair. Trina. He was dreaming, but it was wonderful because it was Trina in his arms. She always did that when they first woke up, scraping her nails along his scalp, arching back against him.

And God, he didn't want to be with her again.

But he wouldn't mind fucking her just one more time.

They'd always...it had always been really fucking good between them.

In his dream, he opened his eyes, wanting to see Trina, but the room was dark enough that he couldn't see more than shadows, couldn't even see his own hand in front of his face.

But he could *feel*.

In this strange dream world, he could feel.

And it was glorious.

He dropped his hand onto Trina's side, skating up to cup her breast through her pajamas. The globe felt larger than he remembered, overfilling his palm, but he didn't stop moving. He continued stroking along her body, slipping his fingers beneath the silky fabric of her clothing.

Sliding them back up.

Over the soft skin of her abdomen, across her ribcage, and then cupping one breast.

Fuck, that was good.

Trina moaned and rocked against him. He slid his free hand down then, scooting it under the fabric of her pajamas. She didn't have any underwear on, which made something blip in his mind. Trina always wore panties to bed.

But this was his dream, and apparently it had granted him a solid by forgoing the extra layer.

His fingers slid through the narrow thatch of hair at the apex of her thighs, slipped along her labia, caressing those soaking folds. Hot and wet and—he slid a finger inside—so fucking tight.

He groaned, thrusting that finger in and out, loving the sound of her moans, her ass rocking into him.

"Fletcher," she breathed, her breath hitching. "Are you awake?"

"Mmm." She didn't sound like Trina, and it made something blip in his mind, but then she rubbed even harder against his cock and he forgot about the voice that sounded different, the slight rasp when it should be softly melodic. He thought of nothing but her body to his, her ass against his dick, and he bent, nipped at her throat, breathing in the musk of her arousal. "I don't care."

"*I* care—"

He slipped another finger in.

She gasped, rocked harder, pussy clamping around his fingers.

"I don't," he muttered, nipping her skin again.

"Fletch—"

He needed to taste her, to be inside her, to fuck her hard and deep, dream or not. Which was why he focused enough as he thrust his fingers deep to say, "I'm with you, baby."

She arched against him. "Mmm. Fletch—"

"I'm going to fuck you so good." He flicked her clit, pumped faster.

"I need—" She grabbed his wrist, yanked it out of her pants. A second later, he was on his back, his shorts were gone, and... best fucking dream ever.

A tight wet sheath surrounded his cock.

He bucked.

"*This,*" she moaned.

Then her palms came to his chest, nails digging in, and Trina gave him a *fucking* ride.

Up and grinding down, her hips bucking, fingers gripping tight, she fucked him until he had to close his eyes against the swirling shadows, the sparks gathering behind his vision, had to squeeze his lids tight just to focus on the pleasure swarming through him. It gathered at his toes and fingertips, burned up his arms and legs, arrowed through his heart, his gut.

Tighter and tighter.

Her pussy clenched around him. His name tumbled from her lips.

She ground down hard, and...he exploded.

Ash and cinder overcome by bliss.

"Fuck, that's good, Trina," he groaned, yanking her down onto his chest as he thrust once, twice more, holding her tightly against him as wave after wave of pleasure flooded him. His head dropped back onto the pillows, his arms flopped to the mattress.

And sleep rose up to tug him back under.

So quickly and completely that he hadn't noticed the woman go still over him.

Nor that sunlight was starting to peek in through the windows.

That the shadows of his dream had warmed into the soft glow of the rising sun.

NINE

Tammy

SHE HELD STILL.

Perfectly, absolutely still.

After the best orgasm of her life, his cock still hard and inside her, Tammy had ice flowing through her veins.

The sex had been incredible.

She'd thought it a dream for a minute, but then she'd woken up and it had been the best part of waking up (yes, she sang that —at least mentally). But she'd hadn't been sure he was awake, so she'd asked, and he'd said he was with her, that he was going to fuck her good in a low, rasping voice that had skated over her skin, flooded her pussy with heat and moisture.

His fingers inside her.

His mouth on her skin.

His hand on her breast.

And...she hadn't thought about it further. Or hadn't thought of anything except chasing the orgasm he'd been building within her, the one that threatened to reduce her to ash, to melt her into a puddle of goo. With all that not-thinking, she'd climbed on top of him, yanked his shorts down, and shoved the monster he had between his thighs inside her—and *God* that had felt good. She'd never been with a guy who made her feel almost uncomfortably full. Fletcher's cock was magnificent.

Which meant that riding them both into oblivion hadn't been difficult.

She'd gotten there.

He had been right on her heels.

And...then he'd called her Trina.

Now his cock was still in her, still hard and pulsing, his cum slowly leaking out from inside her, leaving her pussy and the tops of her thighs sticky from the mixture of their releases.

"Fletch?" she asked when she realized he'd gone still, gone limp.

A snore greeted her question.

What the fuck?

She poked his chest, but he didn't so much as move, as miss a beat of snoring.

"Fletcher," she hissed, gripping his shoulders and shaking him roughly.

The fucker didn't move. He'd ground up into her, held and stroked and plunged into her. And...he'd called her Trina.

"Fuck," she whispered, climbing off him and making a fucking mess of her pajama pants, yanking them up, waddling to the bathroom. She'd given her spare set to Connie, and now this one was stained with cum and—

"Fuck," she whispered again, stripping out of her pajama bottoms, dealing with her business on the toilet, and then going to the sink to spot clean the expensive material.

Trina.

He'd said he was with her.

Then he'd called her *Trina*.

The sick feeling in her gut grew.

She hung up her pajamas, hoping that she'd be able to sneak them into the dryer later, or that they would dry before someone —Fletcher—realized what happened.

Realized?

She couldn't wait for him to *realize!* She had to tell him.

Right?

Maybe...

No.

She had to tell him they'd had sex. That it was his cum staining her pants, sticking to the insides of her thighs. She at least had to tell him she was clean, make sure he was, too. And fuck. Had she just sexually assaulted him? Had he been too asleep to consent?

Fuck, who was she kidding?

There wasn't even something like *too* asleep. He was or he wasn't.

And fuck, now she didn't think that he'd been awake. Which meant that she was the worst sort of person, and she needed to tell him and—

Nausea twisted through her insides.

He'd said he was awake.

He'd touched her first.

So, maybe he'd just drunk too much?

Which...wasn't any better.

Especially since he'd only had two beers and he'd been sober when they'd gone to bed, and she didn't think that he'd managed to get drunk *and* steal the blankets in the last few hours.

So...what now?

"Why?" she breathed, rubbing the ache in her forehead. God, why had she agreed to this in the first place? Now she was a fucking sexual deviant, a rapist, a—

"Okay, Tam," she said, stopping that train of thoughts

before it could overwhelm her. She needed to talk to him, to figure this out. Nothing good came from spiraling and panicking. She splashed some water on her face and stared at herself in the mirror, psyched herself up. "You just need to tell him what happened. Explain that it was a misunderstanding and that you'll do whatever you can to make it right."

What if he wanted to press charges?

What if—

Fuck.

Okay, yeah. She was freaking out. She needed to take another breath and to go back into the bedroom and just tell him, to ask him if he remembered and it would be okay. They were two adults. Things had just taken an odd turn. Tomorrow she'd sleep on the couch because there was no way she'd be going back to sleep that night, even if light wasn't already creeping in through the windows, and she wasn't stressed to fuck and back.

She needed to wake him up right then.

No delaying. No more spiraling.

She walked into the bedroom, poked him in the side, hissed his name.

Fletcher didn't move.

She grabbed his shoulders, shook him hard.

Still, he didn't move. What the fuck? How deep of a sleeper was this guy?

"Fletcher," she said, loud enough to wake the house. Or so it seemed.

But he just snored softly, as though she wasn't shaking him like a rag doll.

Okay, so the man could sleep. What to do? What to do? What to—

Shower first.

Clearly, he wouldn't be waking up anytime soon. She could

take a minute to get organized, get her thoughts together, game-plan with how to wake him up.

Blaring her cell phone by his ear? That might truly wake the house, and despite the light drifting in through the windows, it was still early.

Licking his nose? No. Licking was definitely a bad idea.

Glass of water on his face? Then she'd get Connie's sheets and pillows wet, and it would create more laundry she needed to sneak around to do. Because how was she going to explain wet sheets?

Oh, sorry, Connie. I'm just a squirter.

Or a grown woman who still wets the bed.

Or I'm—

Right. Enough of that. She should shower first. They were all going on the hike in a couple of hours. Tammy should clean up and then go down and make breakfast for everyone. The smell of bacon and coffee might rouse him, and then they could talk about this.

There. That was a plan at least.

And one that meant she could shower first, remove the evidence of their—*her*—actions.

Right.

She grabbed some clothes from her suitcase—jeans, boots, a thermal, and a hoodie. Layers were best because she wasn't the most outdoorsy girl. She'd probably be panting and sweating and peeling her clothes off in no time. Which was clearly a problem she had around Fletcher.

Not that she'd even taken them off.

Not *all* the way off, anyway.

"Ugh, Tammy. Just stop." She cranked on the shower, cleaned up, then got out and dressed quickly. A quick fluff of her hair. A bit of mascara and lip gloss and a couple of strokes of blush so she didn't look like the snow gathered on the tops of the mountains—pale as hell and camouflaging it with the bright, powdery white stuff.

Then she was slipping out of the room and down the stairs.

It didn't take long to get the coffee brewing and even less time to pull out ingredients for her famous breakfast sandwiches (famous because she'd declared them so). Hopefully, Connie wouldn't need the ingredients she was planning on using for anything. Though, Tammy had seen a grocery store not far away.

If she used something that Connie needed, she would do a food run.

She lined cookie sheets with foil, placed the bacon in neat rows on top of it, and then popped the two trays into the oven.

Next was potatoes.

She sliced them thinly, coated them with salt, pepper, and olive oil, and placed *that* tray in the oven. Instead of having to cram a third tray inside the heated chamber, like she'd have to do at home, she had a second oven to load up.

Double ovens.

The height of luxury.

And yes, evidence that she was just a girl from the Midwest. Well, so what? Small things like double ovens excited her.

So did the fact that she could easily get a Baby Yoda martini at Bobby's.

See?

Small things.

Focusing on shoving down her squeeing over the double ovens, Tammy cut thick pieces from a loaf of crunchy-crusted sourdough, prepping them with a little melted butter and layering slices of cheddar cheese on top of them before putting them—and yet another cookie sheet!—into the bottom oven.

Four cookie sheets.

Double ovens.

Yeah, someone could *cook* in this kitchen.

And based on the lasagna and other leftovers from last night, Tammy knew that Connie cooked like a beast in this kitchen.

Right.

On to the eggs.

She cracked them into a skillet, scrambled them with salt, pepper, milk, butter, and cheese. Normally, she'd take orders, ask her eaters how they liked their eggs—over easy, scrambled, sunny side up—but it was early, and she was tired and scrambled was the easiest route.

Humming to herself, she waited until she'd flipped the bacon and it was nearly done before turning on the burner and starting the eggs.

Nothing worse than cold eggs, so she liked to time her breakfast sandwich goodness so all the components were ready at nearly the same time. Plates out, then toast out, the cheese melted, the bread crunchy. Then she layered on the bacon—*lots* of bacon. A heaping scoop of eggs, another slice of bread, and the sandwiches were complete.

But...the kitchen was silent.

And as she stared at four loaded plates, she realized that she might have underestimated the Kings. If his parents slept as deeply as Fletcher, then it would be unlikely that coffee and bacon smells would tempt them out of bed.

She'd practically shouted in his face, had gone full earthquake in his bed.

So why would—

"Is that bacon?" a raspy male voice asked.

Whirling around and nearly upending the plates she'd so carefully made, she watched as Fletcher stumbled his way into the kitchen. No shirt. Those pecs and arms on full display. His hair a fucking mess. He looked thoroughly fucked.

Because she'd fucked *him*.

He blinked, rubbed a hand down his chest. "Tammy—" A shake of his head. "You cooked?"

"I just threw something quick and easy together," she said, picking up a plate and shoving it at him. "Here. Sit. Eat." She pointed at the island, watching as he made his way toward a stool. "Look, Fletch, we need to talk—"

"Is that coffee I smell?" Connie asked, stumbling into the room.

She looked just as wrecked as Fletcher—her hair askew, the pajamas Tammy had loaned her buttoned wrong. Fletch's mom appeared thoroughly fucked as well, and the smirk on Tony's face as he trailed her into the kitchen added credence to Tammy's mental assessment.

"And bacon," Tony said, inhaling deeply. "Oh, my God!" he exclaimed, his gaze coming to the plates in her arms. "Breakfast sandwiches and coffee? You're an angel." He ruffled Tammy's hair. "Thanks, sweetheart. You didn't have to go to any trouble. I usually take the AM cooking shift and Connie the PM."

That hair ruffle made Tammy feel oddly pleased.

But since she couldn't stand there, smiling and pleased with herself because she threw together a couple of breakfast sandwiches, she asked. "What do you guys do for the lunch shift?"

Connie shuffled to the coffee pot and began filling the mugs Tammy had set out. "Fend for ourselves," she said sleepily.

"Lunchables," Tony shared, looking much more chipper than his wife. He moved to the fridge, opened a drawer Tammy hadn't looked in and revealed...

Good grief.

It was *packed* with Lunchables—turkey, chicken nuggets, nachos, ham, the little hot dog ones—and if she'd thought they were joking, that notion had been quickly erased.

"Wow," she breathed.

Fletcher came and took the other plates from her arms, setting them around the kitchen island. "Yup. My parents are elementary school kids at heart."

"Rude," his mom said blearily.

"Because I have a palate?" he teased.

Tammy smiled as Connie handed her a filled coffee mug. "For the record, the chicken nuggets are my favorite," she confided in Fletch's mom.

Connie grinned. "I knew I liked you for a reason."

More pleased feelings. More standing there grinning like a loon.

Her own family was great. There had never been a moment where she didn't know she was loved, that they didn't have her back. But...she was the youngest, the one who often felt like an afterthought. The accident. The unwanted fourth sibling.

Not fair, she knew. Her parents loved her.

But it was also the truth.

Tammy *had* been an accident. She'd heard that stated more than a handful of times over the years, the baby that came after her dad got snipped. The baby who made her mom cry when she'd found out she was pregnant because she didn't want another kid. The fetus responsible for making her mom vomit every single day—several times a day—for the entire nine months (or the *eternal* forty weeks, as her mother liked to declare) of pregnancy.

It was a family joke.

It...didn't feel good.

Oh, boohoo, Tammy, her inner voice said. *You have a loving family who teases you occasionally. Such a tough life.*

Right.

She pushed the bit of moroseness aside, focused on the shirtless man she'd just fucked, and wondered again how in the hell she was going to tell him what had happened.

And yeah, that made her feel *so* much better.

But then Connie patted the stool next to her. "Come sit and eat, honey. Before it gets cold."

And Tammy knew she could stay in her head, could continue to worry about what went down with Fletcher, or...

She could eat her sandwich while it was hot.

She could...procrastinate.

Yeah, that sounded better.

Tammy took her plate and sat next to Connie.

TEN

Fletcher

THE BREAKFAST SANDWICHES were the best thing he'd ever put in his mouth.

His parents seemed to feel the same, devouring their eggs, bacon, and butter-and-cheese covered bread with relish.

The only one who was moving a little slower was Tammy.

She picked at her sandwich and when he came enough out of his Hoovering haze to be aware of anything except that he was still half-asleep and his stomach was rumbling because he'd smelled bacon, he saw that she had dark circles under her eyes.

Tired.

Because she was regretting this?

A wave of guilt flowed through him.

He'd dragged her up here, brought her to a strange house where clearly, she hadn't slept well because she was up before the sun was fully up and cooking for his family.

No wonder she was tired.

Tammy seemed to realize they were all done—all except

her, anyway—picked up her half-full plate, and started to carry it to the sink.

"No way." His mom hopped to her feet, snagged the porcelain circle. "You two shoo. Go do fun, coupley things."

"Like getting ready for the hike Carrie is going to drag us on?" Fletcher teased.

"She wants to do some sort of woo-woo prewedding ceremony in the woods," his dad muttered, "and drag us on a seven-mile hike while we commune with our inner nature spirits."

Tammy choked. "Seven miles?"

"In snowshoes," his dad said, still muttering.

"Snow," she squeaked, "*shoes?*" Her eyes flew to Fletcher's, and she whispered, "I brought hiking boots, but I didn't bring snowshoes."

Fletcher fought back a grin. "Dad's joking about the snowshoes. At least I think he is. We're only hiking—"

"Seven miles?" she whispered as his dad joined his mom in beginning to wash dishes. "He's joking about that, too, right?"

"Um," Fletch began.

Tammy's face fell.

Shit.

He took her arm, guided her from the kitchen, out through the French doors that led to the small deck that overlooked his parents' back yard. "You can stay—"

"*Seven miles?*" she asked—or rather squeaked—again.

He winced. One could never tell with Carrie. She tended to get a little excited where nature was concerned. Sometimes it was two miles, sometimes it was ten. And he was willing to bet that no one would be begging her to stop or cut the hike short like tended to happen when she usually got carried away. Not when it was her wedding weekend.

"Seven?" Tammy whispered.

All he could do was try to keep his face neutral and shrug.

Tammy groaned.

He'd started to open his mouth to tell her that they'd figure it out, that she could skip out on the hike and he'd cover for her.

But then he heard that groan.

And everything inside him stilled.

That *groan*.

That breathy, soft groan that rumbled down his spine, gathered in his dick, making blood pool there like it had—

In his dream.

In. His. *Dream*.

Oh, holy fuck.

"Tammy," he whispered.

"Seven miles," she was saying again, his grip having slackened to release her arm as she paced away. She shoved her hair out of her face, released a sigh, and straightened her shoulders. "Okay. Seven miles. I can do seven miles. It's fine. I'm going to be fine. Yup, I'm—"

Slick heat.

A tight pussy clamping around his dick

Lush breasts.

That. Groan.

"We fucked."

In the middle of her pep talk about surviving the seven-mile hike that Carrie had planned—hopefully sans snowshoes so as not to make him a liar—his blurting out, *"We fucked,"* froze her in almost comical fashion. Her mouth dropped open, her eyes went wide, and she spun so fast that he was surprised she hadn't rolled up the deck beneath her feet like in a cartoon.

"I—*what?*"

He stepped toward her, closed the distance between them. "Last night. This morning. We fucked, Tammy." Her cheeks went bright pink, and then her face went pale. "I was inside you. Your nails"—he tugged the neck of his T-shirt to the side and glanced down. Sure enough, there were nail marks there, ones he hadn't noticed in his stupor earlier—"marked me. I—"

She clamped a hand over his mouth. "I didn't mean to."

He frowned, peeled her fingers away, starting to ask her whatever the hell that meant.

But she kept talking, and he soon learned.

"You"—a shake of her head—"I asked if you were awake, and you answered. You said you were with me, and I thought... well, I guess I didn't realize how heavy you sleep so when I'd asked..."

He shifted closer. "Was it good?"

She paled further. "I—" Another shake of her head. "Why the hell does that matter?"

He snaked an arm around her waist, tugged her flush against him. "It matters to me. I thought it was a dream"—she winced— "but I thought it was the best fucking dream of my life."

"Right," she murmured and there was something in her tone, something dark, something pained. "With Trina."

His brows drew together. "What?"

"You called me Trina."

Fucking hell.

She smiled, and it was forced. "Well..." She cleared her throat. "Anyway, that's not the point. I'm...I'm sorry that I didn't realize you weren't awake. I feel horrible, and I—"

"It's okay," he whispered.

Her ponytail snapped behind her when she shook her head. "It's not."

"Tam—" he began

"It really isn't okay," she said, stepping out of his arms and shoving a hand through her hair, clenched it tightly. "I should have realized you weren't actually awake—"

"How?"

She blinked. "What?"

"How would you know that I wasn't really awake?"

A frown marred her brow.

"Would you ask me if I was awake?" That frown deepened. Those lips parted. "Of course, you would," he said before she could speak again. "And you'd expect me to answer. Which I did." He cupped her cheek. "I remember every moment. *Every* moment."

"Except you thought it was a dream."

"Like I said, the best one of my life."

Her words were quiet. "Featuring Trina."

"Yes." He had. He wasn't going to lie. "I did think you were Trina." He stifled a grimace. Though he knew the bigger question was why he thought he'd been dreaming of Trina in the first place. He'd had sex with other people. But...not sex that meant anything.

Because they weren't Trina.

And he was startled to realize that none of them were...*Tammy*.

His gaze flicked up in time to see hurt dance across her face. "I...um...I should go get ready for the hike."

"Sweetheart," he began as she backed away.

"No, really." Her smile was forced. "If I'm going to hike seven miles, I'd better put on my good socks." A chuckle that sounded painful. "And find some snowshoes."

He reached for her. "Tam—"

A quick movement had her darting around him, her fingers wrapping around the door handle and pulling.

"Tam—"

She slipped inside, her red hair fanning out behind her, and the door closed with a soft *snick*.

And he was left alone in the quiet on the porch—the sun shining, a gentle breeze shifting the cool air through the tall pines, rustling the needles, drifting across his skin. He'd loved growing up here, loved being able to disappear into the trees (keeping an eye out for bears, of course), but just getting lost in the sensation of being small amongst big, unimportant in the grand scheme of nature.

Usually, it brought him peace.

But that morning, he was left thinking that, once again, he'd fucked everything up.

Seriously, how had he never noticed that Tammy had the best ass?

Rounded, the perfect size to be cupped, stretching that denim in a way that made him desperate to peel down the fabric.

Usually, he saw her in slacks, and not that he hadn't noticed Tammy's ass—he'd be lying if he said he hadn't—he just usually kept it professional and dutifully averted his gaze if he happened to catch a glimpse of...well, *ass*.

Now Tammy had been hiking in front of him for the last hour, and he was having a lot of quality time with her ass in his face.

Add in that it was encased in tight jeans...

And yeah, well, he was just lucky that it was cold outside.

Of course, he'd also like to see her pretty face, those gorgeous eyes, *along* with that lush ass. She just...wasn't showing them to him.

Instead, she was avoiding him.

And doing it in a very sneaky way that had him not realizing she'd been doing that avoiding until they were three miles into their hike.

First, she'd been getting ready, and he wasn't an idiot. She'd obviously been upset over the whole calling out Trina's name thing, upset that he hadn't immediately remembered they'd had sex because he was a fucking bastard and in his head and a heavy sleeper. So, at first, he'd given her space.

Space to dress.

Space to get ready.

Then she'd been commandeered by his mom to help select her Lunchable for the hike.

To which Tammy had countered the Lunchable selection and sent him to the store for supplies. She'd said she would take lunch duty while she was visiting and had proceeded to make enough chicken salad sandwiches with fruit salad for an army.

Prepping and packing those had taken time—not a surprise—and then they'd left to meet Carrie and Sean and their respective bridal parties of honor at the trailhead.

Much exclaiming had commenced about the sandwiches and fruit.

Then they'd gotten on with hiking...and Carrie had claimed her.

Then Sean.

Then she'd claimed his dad.

Then struck up a conversation with Hayley—Carrie's maid of honor.

Right about the time she'd began talking to Jim—Sean's best man—was when he finally clued into the sneaky avoidance. Yes, he was slow. Yes, he'd spent too much of the hike fantasizing about that ass and all the things he wanted to do with it.

So, finally, he stopped enjoying the view and started thinking.

Something he should have done before beginning this whole charade, something he definitely should have done before all the ass daydreaming. And something he certainly should have done after seeing the hurt on her face that morning.

Because Tammy was all talk about not wanting a relationship.

She had to be.

Because otherwise, why would she have been hurt over what had happened that morning?

Because you thought you were dreaming while you fucked her, and—oh—because you called her another woman's name?

Right.

There was that.

But he still thought that she wasn't as firm on not wanting a long-term relationship as she tried to convince everyone she was. Yeah, she wanted to focus on her career—and he wholeheartedly supported that—but she also liked people. She had good friends, was connected to everyone in the office, and her family seemed as loud and brash as his was.

She wasn't a woman who liked to be alone.

No, she wasn't.

And just because she has friends, a good job, and a family means that she wants a boyfriend?

Right. There was that, too.

But maybe she just hadn't met the right man?

And that man is you?

Damn his inner conscience was a brutal motherfucker.

One that spoke the truth, of course, but one that was still brutal. Fletcher had no business thinking that he could change her mind about wanting a relationship, about wanting him. Hell, he should be running from the complication of dating someone from work.

But he didn't *want* to run.

He wanted the complication, wanted to be a stubborn asshole and to be the man to change her mind about wanting to be tied with someone.

To be the right man for *her*.

He smothered a wince at the caveman thoughts and focused on hiking, but between his wince-smothering and his ass-watching he missed the branch flying back toward him—Tammy having pushed it to the side as she hiked.

No sooner had he spotted the branch flying toward him than it was whipping him in the face and knocking him to the ground.

"Fuck," he muttered, rubbing his cheek, lifting his fingers to see them painted red with blood.

If he ended up with stitches for the wedding pictures, his mom was going to kill him.

Tammy and Jim spun around, and he noticed it was several moments after he'd decided to warm the cold soil. It was hard not to be resentful of that delay, especially when he was bleeding and he'd noticed Jim checking out Tammy's ass, too—the bastard.

Yes, he was fully aware that it was hypocritical of him.

But Jim was single and had a roving eye and a love for keeping things light and unconnected with women...and Tammy had herself convinced she wanted that.

More asshole, caveman tendencies.

But he couldn't bring himself to care, not when he finally got a glimpse of those pretty pale brown eyes—along with her kissable lips, her pert nose, her cute chin—as she turned to see what had happened—or more likely, why he'd been grunting and cursing. And then he realized there was a perk to getting knocked on his ass.

Mainly that it got her close to him, eliminated that sneaky avoidance she'd been practicing.

"Shit, Fletcher, are you okay?" She knelt by his side and began running her hands over him. And yeah, that was nice.

And yeah, that made him a caveman asshole.

Regardless, he wasn't about to stop her. No fucking way.

Not when her hands felt good. Not when they were clearing the fog from his mind and making him remember how good those hands had felt on him in his dream—or rather, how good they'd felt during their early morning interlude.

"Damn," she murmured, "it's deep."

That's what she said.

Great. Now his inner voice was turning him into a comedian.

"I'm okay," he said.

Her eyes flew to his, held. "You're *bleeding*."

Concern.

He couldn't lie and say he wasn't eating it up, but Carrie and Sean were slowing ahead, his mom and dad following suit. Soon the hoards would be descending and as much as he liked Tammy fussing over him, he didn't think he'd be able to handle Tammy *and* his mom *and* Carrie fussing.

"I'm good, sunshine," he said, covering her hand and taking it in his own, holding it as he stood, drawing her to her feet at the same time. "Just rub a little dirt in it and call me good."

Tammy scowled. "That is neither sanitary nor funny."

He kissed the top of her head. "Maybe not the first, but it's definitely the second."

"What's the matter?" Carrie called.

"He—" Jim began.

Tammy tugged his arm, turning Fletcher so he was facing away from the bride to be and cut Jim off before he could summon the masses. "Fletch just wanted to show me something about this...um...tree!"

His dad started laughing. Sean got a shit-eating grin on his face. Jim seemed to realize he'd lost any chance of flirting with Fletcher's girlfriend. Carrie and his mom just smiled and started hiking again, his mom calling out over her shoulder, "Be sure to show her the ones just off the path."

Fletch smothered a laugh.

"I'm not going to hear the end of that one, am I?"

"They'll be calling you an arborist before long."

"Hilarious."

"Damn right."

Tammy sighed and shook her head, but as the rest of their group disappeared out of sight, she slipped off the small backpack she was carrying and reached in to pull out a first aid kit.

"Prepared," he murmured.

"Former Girl Scout," she said softly, her fingers gentle as she opened a wipe and swiped at his cheek. It stung, and he hissed out a breath, but then her grip tightened as she held him in place. "I like to be prepared."

"And here you were worried about hiking seven miles," he teased.

"*Still* worried about hiking seven miles. It's been more than two decades since someone got me on a trail. I was much more into the weaving and cookie consuming part of scouting."

"Consuming?" he asked. "I thought the whole point was to sell."

"That's true, but have you ever surrounded yourself with a hundred boxes of Thin Mints? They're impossible to resist. You're like, I'll just have a couple and the next thing you know, you've eaten the entire sleeve."

"Why does that sound dirty?"

Pale brown eyes narrowed. "Because you're disgusting?"

He winked. "There are worse qualities."

A bright red brow arched. "Really?"

Another shrug.

"What are they?"

He paused, pondered that, knowing that she had him backed into a corner as he struggled for a witty reply. Obviously, pedophiles and murderers and war lords were worse than being disgusting and those were just the top three that came to mind. But he didn't want to take the conversation somewhere dark.

She swiped his cheek again.

He hissed again.

She leaned closer, her breath coming to his cheek as she blew lightly on the cut. Then he was hissing out another breath that had nothing to do with the sting of the cleaner and had everything to do with Tammy's mouth, her body being very close to his.

"I win," she whispered, smoothing a bandage over the cut.

"Mmm?" He took the wipe and kit from her, shoved them into her backpack, zipped it closed, and tossed it over his shoulder.

"I win," she repeated, a smirk dancing on her lips. "I made the unflappable Fletcher King speechless."

"Hmm." He fought back a smile. "Not speechless for long."

A shrug. "Length doesn't matter."

"That's what she said."

Tammy rolled her eyes. "Hilarious."

"Why do you think I'm unflappable?" She was enjoying her so-called victory—either that or she didn't appreciate his humor (rude!). Regardless of the scenario, she didn't protest when he laced their fingers together, nor when he started them walking forward again...only this time it was to guide her casually off the path.

"Because you *are* unflappable," she said and shrugged. "Nothing much ever seems to get to you."

Except her.

Tammy got to him.

But he was a mess—or at least felt like a mess—every time he was around her, Fletch considered that supposed unflappable-ness a victory of his own...

And then he guided her a little farther off the path.

ELEVEN

Tammy

"THINGS GET TO ME," he murmured, squeezing her hand, and drawing her forward.

She rolled her shoulders, and they finally weren't aching.

Mostly because Fletcher was now carrying her backpack.

Also because she was still hopped up with adrenaline. When she'd turned and seen him on the ground, worry had knotted her insides. And then when she'd seen the blood on his cheek, her pulse had sped, becoming bullets in her veins, thrumming against her skin.

Scared for him.

Stupid, right?

It had been a small cut. Yes, it was deep—or at least deeper than she'd expected. Yes, it had bled a fair amount.

But she'd been able to wipe the blood away and fix everything with a Band-Aid.

So, it hadn't been bad enough to warrant the fear that had slammed into her.

The relief that had trailed the fear had been a tsunami crashing into her other side.

And now she was reeling when she should still be upset and avoiding. Upset because she wasn't Trina and he'd thought she was, upset that she'd spent the morning thinking she was the worst sort of person for fucking him when he hadn't been aware of what he was doing, and then upset because he remembered.

And...upset because she'd been triggered.

Because she wanted to be the person someone picked.

Which made her feel...

Icky. Weak. Stupid. Pathetic.

Ugh.

She sucked a breath in through her nose, realized she'd been quiet and in her head for too long—something she hated. It was a scary place, her mind. Which meant she needed to get the hell out of it, and—funny story—step one of that was to stop thinking she was weak, stupid, and pathetic.

Ding. Ding. Ding.

Folks, we have a winner!

Releasing a breath slowly, she rewound—rapidly past the negative thoughts—and halted at the last thing that Fletcher had said.

Things get to me.

"What kind of things?" she asked.

"Hmm?" he asked, nudging her slightly so she didn't run into a tree.

And speaking of trees, the path seemed to have closed in on them. The trees were taller, the air cooler, and contrary to where they were hiking before, snow was gathered in little pockets. It coated the base of the trunks, encroached on the narrow trail.

She shivered. "What sorts of things get to you?" she clarified.

Look at her go, staying on target.

Fletcher tugged her hand, but instead of avoiding an obstacle, this time the tug was drawing her to a halt, turning her to face him.

"What?" she asked softly, suddenly aware that it was really quiet.

Had the others picked up the pace so much that they weren't going to catch up?

A thread of concern threaded through her. "Do you know where you're going?" she asked.

Silence had her glancing up and seeing a satisfied smile trail across his face. "I know where I'm going," he said when he caught her staring, the words a heated rasp that slid over her skin. "And"—his voice went a little hard—"one of the things that gets to me is hurting a beautiful, sexy woman." He lifted his free hand, tucked a strand of hair behind her ear.

She shivered again when his fingers trailed over the shell of her ear, down the column of her throat.

"Cold?" he murmured.

Now that she thought of it, she *wasn't* cold. Not in the least. Not even with the snow accumulating along the path. Instead of little pockets around the trees, it was collecting into larger banks, connecting the trunks like a frozen Connect-the-Dots. If it kept up, they were going to need to strap on the snowshoes Fletcher was carrying for both of them.

"Tammy?"

His voice was like silk.

Why was his voice like silk? And why did it make her feel like she was burning up inside? Like she'd melt the snowbank if she sat down in it, ending up soaked and doggy paddling in a puddle.

"Tammy?" he asked again.

Still like silk...but with a touch of velvet that made her

thighs quiver. "Hmm?"

"Are you cold?"

A shake of her head. "No," she said. "I'm not cold."

He slipped his fingers free, slid his arm around her shoulders, drew her close.

She squirmed in his hold. "I said I wasn't cold."

He just held her tighter. "Your lips are blue and you're shivering—"

"I—"

"—and plus," he said like it was no big deal. "I like you in my arms."

Warning. Warning, Tammy Huntington.

"Fletch—" she began.

But didn't finish the -er.

Because suddenly her back was against a tree trunk. Or rather, she was pressed to Fletcher's hands, which were pressed to the tree trunk, and his front was pressed to *her* front, and all that pressing was pretty fucking nice.

Really fucking nice.

Incredible even.

But he was looking at her with gentleness in his eyes, with concern and something that might be longing on his face. It sure as shit wasn't lust or molten heat or whatever the smutty romance novels she preferred called it. This wasn't the face of a man who wanted a quick fuck, something hard and fast and mutually satisfying. Instead, Fletcher's face was *soft*.

More warnings.

More danger.

She was Tammy Huntington, and she didn't do soft or gentle. She wanted to be respected, for sure. To be treated with common courtesy, definitely.

She didn't want soft.

No, because then *she* would feel soft in turn, and that would inevitably end up with her feeling like shit.

She tried again. "Fletch—"

"I see you, Tammy Huntington," he murmured, bending close, his lips on the exposed skin of her throat, the words damp puffs of heat that had her shivering again.

Not because she was cold. Again.

He stepped closer, and cold was the last thing on her mind. Instead, it was the hard heat of his body, the impact of those words on her heart.

I see you.

Her breath shuddered out, and she did the only thing she could. Distraction.

She reached down and shoved her hand into the waistband of his jeans, wrapped her fingers around the hard length of his cock, and—

Found herself jostled as her hand was tugged free, nearly dropped, and then she was pinned again, her hands trapped between their chests, Fletcher's face mere centimeters from hers —so close that she could feel his breath when he said again, "I see you."

And then his mouth was on hers, his body so gloriously close, his tongue in her mouth, his arms wrapped tight as he kissed her until she forgot where she was, forgot the terror of those words, forgot that they had more miles ahead of them. She forgot her name, forgot the cold that wasn't cold. But she didn't forget the feel of his lips on hers, the need that touch invoked, the desire that left her shaking and needy, how good it had felt to have him inside her.

"Fletch," she moaned when he released her lips and began kissing his way across her jaw.

"I see you," he murmured into her ear, tongue laving the lobe, goose bumps prickling along her nape, her arms. He shifted and suddenly, she was straddling his hips, the hard length of his erection rubbing against just the right spot, pressing the seam of her jeans against her clit.

And fuck the man had rhythm.

He'd had it in a dream state.

But it was even better like this—with their breaths rasping through the cool air, his boots crunching in the snow, his mouth nipping and licking and kissing his way from behind her ear, down her throat, and then back up to take her lips again. And not once did he stop the slow grind between her thighs. Not once did he falter in that steady rhythm that was steadily driving her insane.

With pleasure.

So really, there were worse places to be.

"Fletch—" Her voice broke just as she was considering shoving him back, reaching between their bodies again, and getting that hard cock inside her again.

Her voice *broke* because he did something with his hips that should have been illegal.

Something that had her throwing her head back, barely noticing the pulse of pain that came from her skull colliding with the tree.

Fletcher noticed though, his hand snaking up, cupping the back of her head, protecting it, even as his hips continued grinding, and the movement paired with that blip of protection that was fucking kryptonite to all of her shields, sent her flying over the edge.

Need was coiled taut in her womb, and she cried out when it detonated, exploding from her center and filling her with pleasure, making her limbs go lax, her body slump in Fletcher's arms.

His mouth found hers as she tried to catch her breath—making that really difficult—but then she was kissing him and the man was a fantastic kisser and as much as she liked her orgasm, she was feeling very empty and wanting another courtesy of that glorious cock he was hiding in his pants, and—

He shifted, lowering her to the ground for a second, hands on her hips to steady her when she wavered. She was still blinking, still trying to pull herself together when he let her go and she heard fabric rustling. And seriously, thank fuck, the man must be getting naked. But by the time she managed to catch her breath, to peel her lids back, it was to see Fletcher fully dressed, the backpacks strapped to his front.

"I—"

He knelt, turned, and gave her his back. "Up you go."

"Um..."

His fingers wrapped around her wrist, tugged her toward him—or rather, practically over him, since she ended up stumbling forward and falling over his back. Before she could right herself, she was wrapped around him, his palms beneath her thighs, her arms around his shoulders.

"Fletcher, I—"

He gripped her a little tighter, stood, and started walking back toward the trail.

"I see you, Tammy," was all he said.

Those words.

Why did they settle over her like a warm blanket? Why did they make her melt when she should be launching herself out of Fletcher's arms and demanding she walk?

It would be easier to say it was because the orgasm had left her feeling lethargic and weak and too tired to continue with however many miles they had left.

But that would be a lie.

And Tammy might be a lot of things, but she wasn't a liar.

She liked the words.

Liked that he was taking care of her.

Liked...Fletcher.

TWELVE

Fletcher

"MUSSED HAIR, SWOLLEN LIPS," Sean said under his breath, and it was a fucking wonder that the bastard was even able to speak with how big his smirk was. "All you're missing is the misbuttoned clothes."

"Shut up." Fletcher socked him in the arm.

Hard. Though not hard enough to warrant his brother's reaction.

"Ow," Sean whined, clutching his biceps. "I'm going to tell Mom on you."

Fletcher just glared. "You're fine. You're *going* to shut your mouth and not fuck up things for me with Tammy."

"*Did* you fuck things up with Tammy?"

He glanced over his shoulder, stared at the woman who had become his obsession. Her color was high as she talked to Hayley, probably less from the orgasm since that had been nearly an hour before, and more from the fight she'd given him to put her down before they'd caught up with the group.

For close to twenty minutes, it had been perfection.

She'd held tight. He'd enjoyed the hike, the quiet, the feeling of peace and satisfaction of having her pressed to him.

Then she'd seemed to come out of the haze of pleasure.

She'd squirmed. Then she asked to be let down. Then demanded it.

So, he had.

And then she'd taken two steps and nearly ate it.

So, he'd scooped her up again. Cue more fighting, more demanding, more...kissing.

As in, he'd found himself spinning, pinning her to a tree again, and kissing her senseless. Kissing himself senseless in the process, finding himself very close to forgetting why he hadn't fucked her against that tree, even though she would be open to it, even though she *wanted* it.

Even though *he* wanted it just as much. Maybe more because he wanted to prove to her that he wanted her and not Trina.

That Tammy was more and special and—

"No," he said, more to himself than to his brother. Mostly because he'd forgotten that Sean had been talking at all. He needed to rein it in and focus on winning Tammy over.

She wanted him.

She wasn't as allergic to relationships as she made herself out to be.

It was in the pain on her face that he'd caught a glimpse of on the back deck. It was in the way she interacted with his parents, with Sean and Carrie, with Jim and Hayley. It was the regret in her eyes when she'd worried that he hadn't been aware enough to consent. It was the way she was so fucking capable at everything—work, cooking for his family without a blink, getting along easily with this group even though she didn't know them. It was stepping into a situation to help someone that she absolutely didn't have to.

Tammy was attached.

She was just spending a lot of time pretending she wasn't.

"So, why does she look like she wants to throttle you?"

Blinking up at Sean, he frowned as the words processed then turned to glance back at Tammy.

Yup.

Daggers might as well be flying from her eyes.

"None of your business," he muttered.

"Hmm."

"Shouldn't you be paying attention to your soon-to-be-bride?"

"She and Mom are busy."

And they were—spreading out a blanket, unpacking the sandwiches Tammy had made earlier, setting out utensils and the container of fruit salad.

"Don't be an asshole," he muttered. "Help your almost wife."

Carrie glanced up and smiled at his brother. Sean quit with his tormenting and took a step toward his fiancé. Whipped.

Just as bad as Fletcher was.

Attempting casual—and probably not looking casual at all—he sidled his way toward Tammy.

She smelled like fall.

She personified temptation.

She was everything he'd ever dreamed of wanting.

He slipped an arm around her waist, slid close, and though she went stiff, she didn't push him away. Probably because Hayley was there, because his family was surrounding them, and maybe it made him an asshole, but he was soaking up any inch she was giving him, so he didn't move away, just held her a little tighter, inhaled the scent of her hair.

Narrowed eyes on his. "Did you just sniff me?"

A shrug. "Maybe."

More narrowing. "Why?"

"Because you smell good."

She snorted. "You've lost your mind."

"Maybe." He sniffed again.

Her eyes were wide when she gazed up at him. "Fletcher," she said on a chuckle.

He bent, nuzzled her ear. "I like you, Tammy Huntington. A whole lot." Straightening, he saw the panic in her eyes, dipping into the lines of her face, watched the shield slide in place over her features. "Don't worry," he said.

A deep V between her brows. "About what?"

About so many things—the least of which being the fact that he wasn't going to stop liking her, that he was going to get Tammy to like him too, that he was going to maybe do more than just liking—and do that soon—but because just him declaring he liked her had her freaking out, he was going to keep that last bit of information to himself.

"Anything," he murmured. "Don't worry about anything."

Her frown deepened. "I—"

And just because he could, because he couldn't stop himself, because he thought he might die if he didn't do it, Fletcher closed the distance between their mouths and kissed her.

Deeply.

Her lips were unmoving against his.

At least until he touched his tongue to the seam of her mouth. Then they parted and he found himself drawing her closer, tangling his fingers into her hair, deepening the kiss. She released a breath, or maybe it was a moan. Either way, it flowed from her mouth to his, dancing across his tastebuds, overfilling them, marking them, scorching them, changing them forever.

Tongue and teeth and lips.

Soft breasts, firm thighs, sharp nails biting into the muscles of his arms.

Silken hair, breathy moans, and...

A sharp smack on the back of his head.

"Didn't you get enough alone time in the trees?" his dad muttered.

Fletch was slow to emerge from the fog that only Tammy seemed to be able to create, even slower to process the words his dad was saying. But the hardest thing was to tear his mouth free, to release her, to keep his fucking hands and tongue to himself.

They had witnesses.

He couldn't fuck her here.

As much as he wanted to.

"Go on," he murmured when he was finally able to break away, nudging Tammy toward the blanket and the food that was laid out, somehow able to make his voice sound almost normal, even though his lungs were screaming and his dick felt as though it had been turned into some robot dick that never got soft, or like he'd OD'd on Viagra. "You should eat."

She glanced up at him, lips swollen and tempting him. He wanted to kiss her again. Especially when she asked, her expression a bit befuddled, her eyes soft, her pupils dilated, "Eat?"

"Go have a sandwich, sweetheart," he whispered, taking her hand and bringing her to the blanket. "Then it'll be time to get the snowshoes on."

The haze began to clear. "Oh, God. The snowshoes."

His mom took Tammy's hand, tugged her down onto the blanket—yes, they were having a picnic in the middle of the woods in early winter, snow just up the mountain ahead of them. But then again, this was Carrie and Sean's weekend and if there was anything the two of them loved more than each other, it was nature. They'd met on a ski lift as kids. Been best friends for years—hiking, boating, rafting, backpacking, rock climbing, mountain biking. If there was an outdoor activity to be tried, they did it.

And every year they skied every day they could.

Which was why Fletcher's brother had proposed at the top of their favorite black diamond.

"The snowshoes sound scarier than they are," he heard his mom say as he grabbed a sandwich and slipped from the clearing. His dick was throbbing, pushing against the zipper of his jeans, and since he really didn't want to be sporting a boner in front of his family, he slipped away and leaned against a tree, well away from the circle, soaking in the cool air—and hoping it would all go to his cock so the fucking steel rod in his pants would go away—and tried to settle himself.

Because the one thought raging through him was that Tammy Huntington needed to be his.

Only slightly tempered because *he* also needed to belong to her.

Not because of Trina or the chemistry or the most erotic dream/experience of his life.

But because now that he'd gotten a glimpse of the unguarded vulnerability in Tammy's heart, the sweet and caring center, the way she could charm and joke and slide so easily into his life...he couldn't imagine a future without her.

It was funny. He'd known he'd liked her, known he'd respected her, but after that first day at the office—the way she'd reacted when he'd asked her to the work crew Happy Hour—there had understandably been a wall between them.

Reinforced by steel and concrete and barbed wire on her side.

Solid on his because he didn't want to overstep.

Now there was a door in that wall.

One he could unlock, could push open.

THIRTEEN

Tammy

SHE SNIFFED.

And wiped a tear away.

Seriously, why did she always get so emotional at weddings?

Well, truthfully, this wasn't a wedding. It was a centering ceremony complete with sage burning and candles being lit and placed in the four cardinal directions. The ceremony itself was more meditation than actual pomp. But it was still beautiful—Carrie having them all sit down on the blanket again, breathing deeply, and then closing their eyes and soaking in the nature around them.

At first, Tammy had only been able to soak in the fact that her ass was freezing, sitting on that blanket.

It had been cold when they'd stopped for lunch, but there hadn't been any snow where they'd eaten, and though the ground had been cool, it wasn't like sitting on snow.

Eventually, she came to terms with the fact that the cold wasn't going anywhere, but also that the cold wasn't a wet cold.

It didn't soak through the blanket. Her ass may be frozen, but it wasn't wet.

Winning.

And then, as Carrie continued talking, it became less about the cold and her frozen limbs and more about love and joy and happiness—of a present that was so jam-packed with those things that it threatened to explode the confines of reality, of a future filled with life blasting past that reality time and again.

She spoke of tough times and easy ones, of a love that sometimes hurt.

But even those hurts were made easier because they had each other.

Most times, Tammy didn't miss having another half—especially when she understood the risks that such a partnership wrought—but weddings were always tough, the prospect of happy marriages even more so. She had the example of her parents, her brothers, knew that HEAs could happen.

Just...it was a scary fucking idea.

And the one time she thought that she might have found her person—

Fingers on her cheek.

Her eyes flew open, and she saw Fletcher's hand, his thumb glistening with another tear she hadn't realized had escaped. He reached forward and wiped again, this time the other cheek, and then lightly brushed his lips over the damp skin.

Goose bumps on her nape, a strange pounding in her heart.

Something like...longing.

Oh fuck.

She couldn't think about that right now. It was just...yeah, no, she couldn't think about *that* without freaking the fuck out, and she didn't think Carrie would appreciate that during her centering ceremony.

Running screaming through the snow, knocking candles

over, potentially starting a forest fire in her idiocy?

Yeah, that wouldn't be the greatest.

Fletch slipped an arm around her shoulders, brought her close to his side.

And somehow that quieted the panic.

Loosened her lungs, slowed her pulse, made it so that her skin didn't feel like it was three sizes too small.

This was stupid.

She should pull away.

But by then Fletcher's warmth was soaking into her side, and it felt so good that she didn't move away.

Instead, she found herself giving him more of her weight.

Leaning into him and closing her eyes again.

And listening to Carrie's soft words of love and fulfillment.

Until they flowed over her with such force that she began to wonder if perhaps such a thing was possible for her after all.

Began to *wish* it was.

"And then you'll stop here, Hayley will fix your dress, and take your bouquet," Connie was saying, having stepped into the role of wedding planner extraordinaire.

Hayley pretended to take the bouquet, to fluff the wedding dress Carrie would be wearing the next day, and then stood in the spot indicated for her role of maid of honor. The other woman did it with joy in her eyes for her friend, and Tammy couldn't help but miss her own friends.

Connie propelled the ceremony forward and the happy couple proceeded through a shortened version of the "We have gathered here todays" and the vows they would be exchanging.

"Jim," Connie said once that was done. "Do you have the rings?"

"I—uh—right this moment?" he replied, clearly missing the part where he was supposed to be pretending this was the real thing.

Hayley rolled her eyes, the nonverbal, *Men, sigh,* obvious.

Connie sighed, and her *Men, sigh* wasn't kept in her mind or on her face. It was spoken out loud.

Jim cringed.

"You'll have the rings tomorrow?" Connie asked sharply, and the only answer one could give—and still want to live —was yes.

Luckily, even though Jim might not be keen for pretend play, he was a smart cookie.

He answered without preamble. "Yes."

See? Smart man.

Connie stared at him with narrowed eyes.

"Yes," he repeated. "I'll definitely have the rings tomorrow. I —uh—" He patted his pockets, pulled out a keyring, and quickly shifted the keys around until he had two of the silver rings free. "I have these now!"

Connie's eyes softened slightly as he handed the silver keyrings to Sean.

Who grimaced.

"Thanks, man," Sean stage whispered, "don't worry about her. She'll chill once I get a couple of lemon drops in her at the rehearsal dinner."

Connie huffed. "I will not—"

"And *that's* enough, sweetheart," Tony said, swooping in and winding an arm around her waist. "You guys will do the ring exchange thing"—he waved a hand with a casualness that Connie wholly didn't support based on the outraged gasp she released (and that Tony caught on his tongue with a kiss that was very much not wedding appropriate)—"then you'll do the kissing thing—"

"Hopefully with as much passion as you two," Hayley whispered, and Tammy had to bite back a giggle because she'd been thinking the exact same thing.

She wanted someone to love her as much as Tony and Connie loved each other.

With love and passion and bickering and joy and...

With everything.

It was just...no one had ever truly chosen her.

Not *her*. Not Tammy.

Not as a baby or a young woman.

Not now.

Because you push them away.

Maybe she did.

No. She *knew* she did. Other women were fine. Co-workers —not the sleazy trying to get in her pants type—were fine. Men were fine. So long as they didn't get too close. So long as they didn't get attached.

So long as *she* didn't get attached.

Right. *That* was the truth she preferred to keep tucked down. *Way* down.

Buried in the Mariana Trench down.

"And then we'll all cheer and high five," Tony declared, "and you'll walk down the aisle as man and wife—"

Connie swatted him. "Husband and wife," she grumbled. "Women aren't the only ones with the title."

"Husband and wife," Tony corrected without missing a beat. "Then pictures and food and drinking all the lemon drops you want." He kissed the tip of Connie's nose.

Connie swatted him again. "Then pictures, cocktail hour, food, speeches, dancing, bouquet toss, garter toss, cake cutting, and *then* drinking all the lemon drops."

Tony, in all his infinite husband smartness didn't roll his eyes—though his expression seemed to be indicating that he wanted to. Still, he held it back and just nodded. "After all of that," he agreed, "then lemon drops. But for tonight, we're done with this, and it's time to go to dinner."

Connie's eyes went wide. "We really should go over everything one more time—"

"It's just walking up and down the aisle," Tony began. "The kids have it."

Connie started sputtered. "It-it's ju-just *walking?*" Her jaw clenched. "There's the music they have to time their steps to, and the flower girls have to know the proper way to distribute their petals, and I still haven't taught Sean the proper way to hold Carrie's arm so he doesn't step on her train and—"

Carrie stepped down off the altar and leaned close to the side Tony hadn't sidled up to. "Connie?" she asked, linking their arms together.

"Yeah, honey?" Connie asked, sweet as pie.

"I'm really hungry."

Connie snapped to attention—or rather, since she'd been at full attention from the moment they'd all entered the small church, she relaxed marginally.

Okay.

She didn't relax. Not in the least.

Instead, she turned off wedding planner extraordinaire and turned on Mom Mode Extraordinaire.

One movement had her wrapping a hand around their linked arms. Another had her drawing Carrie down the aisle. "Let's go!" she called. "No more delaying. The bride is hungry, and we need to go before we're late for our reservation! Hustle, people. Hustle!"

"She's a loon," Fletcher whispered.

"I don't know if I should be proud or amazed or frightened," she whispered back.

He stepped closer, and she had had bite back a shiver. Or

maybe it was a groan, especially when him being near meant that she remembered the orgasms he'd given her. Dangerous, dangerous man. "All three," he murmured, and when he spoke the words in her ear, she found that this time she couldn't hold back the shiver that rolled through her frame, not when the words puffed over her skin, not when he was so near.

She tried to step away, but he merely followed her, his arms coming around her, his mouth staying near her ear. "We should catch up to them."

Teeth on her lobe. "In a minute."

Her lips parted on a moan, fingers somehow finding their way to his hair. Holding him to her.

When she should be backing away.

Dammit!

His tongue slid out, caressed over her ear.

More shivering.

More dammit.

"You're overstepping, King," she muttered.

"Your fingers are in my hair, holding me to you," he murmured against her jaw. "You like it."

"I don't," she said immediately because...pride and all that.

Another flick of that tongue. "Admit it, Huntington. You. Like. It."

It took everything in her to hold back her shudder, and she had the feeling that he knew she was practically biting her tongue off in order to not melt in his hold. She sniffed. "You wish."

A nip to her throat. "I *know*."

Cocky. So damned cocky.

And why was all that cocky so damned attractive? Hmm? Probably because she'd had the damn man's *cock,* and it was fucking good and—

Fuck it.

She tore away from him.

"Tam—" he began, his eyes filled with concern.

Concern she didn't bother addressing. Instead, she grabbed his hand, and began dragging him toward the side door. She'd been in and out that door more than a half dozen times as she'd helped Connie bring in various things for the wedding the next day. Those boxes were currently stacked in the hall she was dragging Fletcher through.

Because though she wasn't particularly religious, she drew the line at liaisons in a church.

And she and Fletcher were damned well going to have a liaison.

Right this moment.

Just not in a house of God.

She pushed through the door, led him through the vine-covered arbor and into the trees, to the bench she'd rested at in between one of her many trips.

"Sweetheart," Fletcher said, his brows furrowed, "is everything—"

No. *Nothing* was okay. This was supposed to be a silly pretend weekend with no strings, and instead it had become something more. She liked him, and not just his body. He had flaws and owned up to them. He was easy with affection and praise and his family was really fucking cool. It was easy to pretend she fit in here. Easy to acknowledge that she wanted more.

But it was going to end. And she didn't want to think about that, didn't want to think about wanting something that was more than sex.

She wanted an orgasm, a fuzzy mind, to get lost in the bliss of the moment.

And then, come Monday, to pretend that none of this ever happened.

FOURTEEN

Fletcher

HE DIDN'T EVEN FINISH ASKING if she was okay before Tammy launched herself into his arms, mashing their mouths together so hard that he nearly bit his tongue off.

But before he could pull away, her fingers slid into his hair, angled his head and the kiss went explosive.

Maybe it was the ache in his tongue.

Maybe it was the answering ache in his cock.

All he knew was that Tammy kissed him until he couldn't see straight, couldn't feel anything except the lush curves of her body, couldn't process the cold, the darkening sky, the whisper of the breeze.

It was Tammy and *only* Tammy.

She pushed him slightly, and he found the backs of his knees against something hard. Another push had him dropping onto a bench, Tammy's mouth still pressed to his, her tongue delving deep, her fingers gripping tight.

His lungs were on fire.

His hands had somehow found their way to her ass, were

pulling her toward him, trying to get Tammy into his lap so he could do all the things he wanted to her.

But she was slipping out of his hold, loosening her fingers from his hair, and...

Dropping to her knees in front of him, her hands going to the waistband of his jeans, flicking open the button and tugging down the zipper.

He reached for her. "Tam—"

She pulled out his cock and sucked it deep into her mouth.

"Oh, fuck," he groaned, gripping the bench, using every bit of his control to not thrust into her mouth. He could feel himself hitting the back of her throat, didn't want to gag her, but fuck, it felt incredible, and he wanted more, wanted deeper, wanted—

She dragged her teeth up the length of his cock, laved the underside with her tongue.

His groan was torn out of him and probably loud enough to echo through the granite of the mountains, but he was beyond caring. Not when she added her hand, twisting and gripping tight. Not when her tongue and teeth continued working him.

Not when—

More teeth and then suction.

And Fletcher knew he was a hairsbreadth away from losing it.

Somehow, he summoned the inhuman strength to reach for her, to tug her off his cock when he wanted desperately to come in her mouth. But he wanted to come inside her more, *needed* to come in her.

Awake.

Not in a dream.

Just him and Tammy and—

He brought her toward him, sending her clambering onto his lap. Her dress pooled around their waists, and he could feel the heat of her pussy through the dampened fabric of her panties as they brushed over him, once, twice—

Fletcher snaked his hands up and yanked at them, tearing the delicate lace material off one hip, bunching the fabric to the side so she could rub wet heat over him.

Teasing.

Desperate.

Her. *Him.*

Grabbing at her hips again, drawing her up enough to position himself at her entrance. Then he shifted, lifted his hips at the same time he brought her down...and he was home.

They both froze, moans tumbling off their tongues.

Tight and hot, clasping him in a rhythm that threatened to send him out of control, the urge to thrust and fuck and pound into her nearly overwhelming. But he wanted her to know this meant something to him, that he was with her, and her alone.

So...slow and gentle.

Rocking first, grinding into her. Holding her close and guiding her into a rhythm that was controlled and easy, like they had all the time in the world, even though they obviously didn't. Even though someone could easily stumble onto them. Even though they shouldn't be doing this right now, not with the rehearsal dinner happening, not with Sean and Carrie's day being more important than an orgasm.

But this wasn't just an orgasm.

This was Tammy.

This was him showing her that he wanted her. *Her.* Not someone else.

Just the sexy, sweet, funny woman who he liked a whole hell of a lot.

So, he went slow. One hand on her hips, holding her as she moved on him, the other cupping her cheek, running a thumb across her bottom lip. "Tammy," he murmured and bit back a groan when she clenched around him, began rocking faster. "*Baby.*" He dropped his mouth to hers, kissed her deeply. "Fuck, you feel so good," he told her when they broke apart to breathe. "You're so fucking good, baby—"

He choked.

Because she all but leaped off his lap. The cold air hit his cock—hence the choking—and then he was watching Tammy back away from him.

Dread began coiling in his stomach, but before it could truly gather, before he could even ask if he'd been wrong, if she didn't want this, if this was too much too fast, she was bending over the bench. One hand on the cool stone. The other reaching for the hem of her dress.

Tugging it up.

Baring her ass and spreading her thighs, giving him a glimpse of a swollen, glistening pussy.

"Well," she said, glancing back at him over her shoulder, "are we both coming?"

His breath caught. His cock somehow grew harder.

"Come back here and we will."

"I'm tired of doing all the work," she teased and tugged her dress a little higher, spread her legs a bit wider. "I want you to come here."

And like he could deny her anything.

He pushed off the bench, closed the couple of feet between them.

"Inside," she ordered, thrusting her hips back, getting his cock wet again.

Fletcher slid home, and fuck she was tight from this angle. She squeezed him almost painfully and then began moving against him, shifting forward, slamming back hard.

"Fuck me," she said, another order. "Fuck me now and hard, Fletcher. I need it. Please," she said and the intensity, the command had disappeared. Instead, it was full of pleading. "Please, Fletcher. Please, fuck me hard."

He slid an arm up her front, shoved his hand into the bodice of her dress, massaging her breast, pinching her nipple.

Probably a bit too hard, but she wanted hard.

And when he used his other hand to grip her hip, when he began fucking her furiously, obliging her when she demanded he go deeper, thrust faster.

It wasn't soft and sweet and gentle.

It was rapid and brutal and intense.

It was still the best sex of his life, but it wasn't emotional. It wasn't deep.

Well, he was fucking her deep, but he didn't feel this in his heart, was hard-pressed to capture anything other than sensation, pleasure, desire, and need. Primal, basic need that had him forgetting about emotion, about soft and sweet.

Tammy was moaning, her head tossed back, red hair flowing over her shoulders, pale brown eyes hooded and filled with fire, bright white teeth biting into a lush bottom lip.

"Fuck, Tammy," he gritted.

She was so fucking beautiful. "Yes," she moaned, bucking her gorgeous ass against him, "*fuck* Tammy."

So, he did.

He massaged her breast, rolled her nipple, continued to pound into her. And it didn't take long for him to focus on nothing other than giving her the best fucking orgasm of her life.

Sliding out, slamming back in.

Releasing her breast and slipping a hand between her legs.

Vision going blurry as he sought the spot, the rhythm, the touch that made her squeeze even tighter around him, that had her crying out, her head thrown back, moans tumbling from her lips. "Yes. *Yes*. Right there"—she reached down, pressed his fingers more firmly against her pussy, coaxing them to circle her clit—"Oh, God. Yes, Fletch. Right *there.*"

He kept his hand where she wanted it, continued pressing and circling, moving in and out, feeling his own release creep up his spine, start to spiral outward.

Fuck.

It was spiraling fast.

Sweat prickled down his spine, his lips went numb, and he felt almost dizzy as he focused on one thing, and one thing only: getting Tammy to come before he did.

"Fletch—*oh, God.*"

His vision began to blur, his fingers cramp, and—

She went ramrod stiff for a heartbeat and then melted as she came, his name a gasp, her pussy a tight clasp around his cock, milking him and drawing him that last little bit of the way over the edge as his own release surrounded him.

For a second, it felt as though he'd been swimming and was tugged sharply underwater—a la scary as shit *Jaws* vibes—vision blacking out, lungs without air, body feeling like it had been yanked beneath the surface of reality. But just as quickly, he emerged, propelled up through that viscous layer of thoughts, flying through into fresh air, into real life, into wave after wave after *wave* of pleasure crashing into him.

He'd been wrong. It wasn't just physical, even though she tried to make it that way.

It was the dream.

It was so much more.

It was *everything.*

"Tammy," he said, reaching forward and turning her head so he could meet her eyes. "*My* Tammy."

Something flared on her face, in those pale brown depths, and then her lids slid closed, her lips parted on a breath as she slumped down onto the bench.

Fletcher caught her, dragged her close to his chest.

His heart thundered, absolutely thundered against his ribcage, and his skin felt like it was on fire. Every single muscle in his body was strained, having long since gone limp.

Except the ones keeping her to him.

And the muscle working the hardest?

His heart.

FIFTEEN

Tammy

THIS HAD BEEN A MISTAKE.

A serious miscalculation on her part.

Why had she thought fucking Fletcher would cure her of any feelings she had for him?

Oh yeah, because it had always worked in the past.

Seriously, she was a dumb ass. None of her usual tactics were going to work when it came to Fletcher King. She should know that by now. Nothing had been usual. Nothing had gone to plan. It was all fucked, had been from the moment she'd agreed to help him with the wedding, pretending it was just doing a favor for a coworker.

Fletcher had always been more than a coworker, even though she'd tried to tell herself otherwise.

It was in how she reacted to that invitation the first day.

The coldness she'd treated him with after that.

If she were being truly honest, she'd known he wasn't a creeper, even newly meeting him. It was just safer and more convenient to despise him.

Especially when he made her feel...

All the wrong things.

But now, after sex in which she'd tried to deliberately erect some distance between them, she found herself falling even further in with him.

Because it had been hard and fast and intense as hell.

And it had been perfect and soulful and...the way he'd rasped out, "My Tammy," his fingers on her jaw, his eyes boring into hers...it had shattered right through any protections she'd erected. She'd wanted him to continue doing that forever.

He'd looked at her like she was worthwhile.

Like she could be his forever.

She...wanted to be.

Fuck.

He was still inside her and instead of wanting him to leave, to give her space, to pull out so she could put herself to rights and pretend that what had happened between them was just an absolutely scorching orgasm, she wanted him to stay inside her, to keep pumping, to extend the moment. She wanted to not have an IUD, to not have used condoms because they were building a family, a future, rather than just because she was stupid and too turned on to think straight.

And *that* more than anything had her drawing away, closing her eyes, and feigning exhaustion.

Even though fight or flight hormones were pumping through her veins. Even though adrenaline coursed through her —because she was so fucking stupid thinking about making babies when she should be thinking about her job, about making a name for herself, about proving she was just as much of a Huntington as her mom, her siblings.

Not just an HR clerk.

But someone who was changing the landscape of her company, of the industry.

She wasn't saving animals' lives or taking a company public or starting a billion-dollar company like her siblings or mom.

Her life was great. She worked hard.

But at the moment, she wasn't doing anything spectacular.

She wasn't making that difference she wanted to be making.

She was just Tammy, an assistant HR specialist, who was just starting to get her career where she wanted it to be.

Which was why she shouldn't be thinking of making babies.

Tell that to yourself when you're not being ridden bareback, the man's sperm dripping down your thighs.

Smothering a wince, she forced herself to acknowledge that, yes, that had been stupid, and that, no, she wouldn't be doing that any longer.

That being fucking Fletcher King within an inch of both of their lives.

Work first. Career first.

No entanglements.

Said while the man who was creating *all* the entanglements was still hard and inside her.

Never let it be stated that she wasn't hypocritical.

Cute.

"Sweetheart." Warm, calloused fingers on her cheek. How did he have callouses? He worked in an office just like her, and it wasn't like she was getting roughened fingertips from typing on her computer all day and night.

And *that* was an aside she shouldn't be thinking about.

Not with him hard and inside her and—

God, seriously. She needed to stop thinking about the man's cock and the man's hands and the man himself and—

Those fingers drifted down, and he wrapped his arm around the front of her chest and slowly tilted her so she was upright. Then his other stayed at her hip, and she released a sigh of displeasure—

Fuck, come on!

Displeasure? *Really?*

But he was so fucking gentle when he pulled out of her, and when that made a bigger mess between her legs, he simply released her, and set her on the bench. Then he tugged his sweater over his head, dragged off the T-shirt he wore beneath, and then used the material to clean her up.

"I should have used a condom," he said, leaning back on his heels and staring up at her. And God, why did the man have to look like a fucking movie star? She wanted to count his ab muscles like a toddler practiced their numbers—*one, two, three-four-five, I wish I caught a fish alive, six, seven, eight-nine-ten, then I threw him back again.*

No, he didn't have a ten-pack, but he had six yummy squares she wanted to trace with her tongue.

One, two, three-four-five-six.

That didn't have quite the same rhyme to it.

And—oh God—she was really losing it.

One cock, three glorious orgasms, and a man being nice to her, and she was losing her fucking mind.

Buck the fuck up, Huntington. This weekend means nothing. Fletcher means nothing.

It will all go back to normal on Monday—

"I'm sorry I didn't protect you."

Crack.

She practically felt the wall around her reverberate with the impact of his words.

It teetered on the edge of a precipice, its top wavering, the once solid concrete transforming into a stack of bricks that had lost their mortar, lost their combined strength. That undulation began at the highest portion, and it vibrated through the height, shuddering, shifting, and...

Collapsing.

Her heart, along with the noise of that collapse, were both so loud in her ears she was surprised Fletcher didn't hear it, shocked that it didn't blow back the branches of the trees, knock the pine needles off and onto the ground.

It was like an explosion had happened.

Only it was just inside her head.

I'm sorry I didn't protect you.

How? How did he know that was the thing she most wanted to hear?

My Tammy.

Maybe the second most thing she was desperate to hear.

Because *My Tammy* took the cake.

"I'm clean," he said. "I just had my had my physical last week. All the blood work came back clear, but if you're not on birth control—"

"I have an IUD. I'm clean. Got tested just this week. After —" She cleared her throat as he finished wiping her thighs, bunching the T-shirt in his hand. "After the scene you saw at my house, I knew I needed to start fresh, and I always do that with a clean bill of health." She lifted her chin as he straightened the skirt of her dress, half-expecting all the soft and protective to have disappeared, derision in its place. "I also don't normally have sex without a condom."

Never.

She'd never had sex without a condom.

Except with Fletcher.

The remains of the wall inside her mind, her heart, shifted, burping up dust and debris like a dragon breathing fire.

"Smart," he said, stroking his hands down her calves before reaching for his sweater and pulling it over his head. "And I'm glad. Not that I wouldn't take care of you if that happened, but I'm not normally a man who does this without checking that you're protected." Fierce eyes on hers. "So, I'm sorry."

"It's my fault—"

"It's not like I tried to stop the event from happening," he said.

"I instigated."

A shrug, one half of his mouth tipping up. "I happily went along with what you were instigating."

"I've slept with a lot of people," she pressed, not sure why she was pushing this except that she was probably trying to find another angle to retreat, especially with her heart so open and vulnerable. "I should know better."

This is where the derision should circle back and return in full force. But instead, his eyes stayed fierce and his expression soft. "*I* should have known better."

God, why did this man make it so hard to push him away?

Because you don't want to.

Judgy bitch in her mind.

She sighed, glanced out toward the trees. The arbor had tiny twinkling lights woven through it, glimmering in the evening. It had grown quite dark, the sky more navy than sky blue overhead, the planets and the stars shining—though clouds hung over the half-sphere of the atmosphere like diaphanous curtains, softening the light. The entire scene had become ridiculously romantic and if not for the chill creeping into the air, sinking into her bared legs, her exposed arms and chest, she might have thought about a round three.

Only this time, soft and gentle with Fletcher taking her on a bed of pine needles, condom or not.

Or not.

She might as well make it a trifecta.

See? Losing. Her. Mind.

"Come on," he murmured, tugging her up to her feet, slipping an arm around her waist, and drawing her into his side. "Let's get your coat and go meet everyone for dinner."

She groaned.

"What?" he asked, leading them back down the path and toward the church.

Also, side note: now that she wasn't writhing with desire, with a desperate need to pretend nothing inside her had changed, she realized that she was probably going to hell for fucking in the churchyard, even though she hadn't actually boned Fletcher in the church itself.

She was pretty sure that God didn't appreciate premarital sex anywhere on her (yes, *her*—Tammy said it, okay?) grounds.

"What?" Fletcher asked again. "What's that groan for?"

"They're all going to know what we were doing," she moaned.

"You mean because you have just-been-fucked hair?"

Another groan. "Yes, because of *that* exactly."

He lightly tugged a lock of her hair and tucked it behind her ear. "They'll know. They won't care."

"But they'll still know," she muttered as he tugged open the church door. She hesitated on the threshold and carefully stepped over, half-expecting to be smote (smitted? smitten?) Ah, fuck it. That didn't matter. Not when her sinning foot had already hit the pale red carpeting. When she wasn't reduced to ashes, she walked forward with Fletcher, bypassing the altar and the pews as he led her to the closet where they'd stored their coats earlier (and seriously, good man for remembering them because she was freaking freezing now). "And now," she whispered as he held up her jacket so she could shrug into it—whispering because the priest might still be around and she didn't need another religious crisis on her hands if he overheard their sexual escapades, "we're missing part of the rehearsal dinner because I needed an orgasm courtesy of Fletcher King and—"

He tugged her hair again.

"What?" she snapped.

"They'll know," he said again. "They won't care."

"I—"

He bent enough so their gazes could meet, his eyes close to hers, his expression equal parts amused and intense. "They. Won't. Care," he repeated. "You make me happy. That's the only thing that matters. So, we miss some appetizers. Locata's fried cheese is delicious, but you're a thousand times better—"

"Fried cheese?" she moaned. "Everyone's going to know we were fucking like bunnies on the church's grounds, *and* we're missing *fried cheese?*"

That wasn't quiet at all.

Hell, she was practically shouting about their boning good time. She might as well have hollered for the priest and confessed there and then. She was so freaking smooth. And yes, she was mentally rolling her eyes. So much for her trying to be discreet.

Fletcher shrugged into his coat. "I don't think fried cheese can compare to a Fletcher King orgasm."

"You don't know how much I like cheese."

His fingers were on the collar of his jacket, and her statement had him freezing.

Then something wonderful happened.

Something that made a giant vacuum appear in her mind—or maybe a huge sinkhole opened up. Either way, all that debris and dust and crumbled remnants of that wall disappeared.

And she was left wide open.

But his laugh—that wonderful laugh—it rolled over her, filled her up, encased her exposed and vulnerable heart in a protective bubble.

Open.

Exposed.

Safe.

That was her with Fletcher King.

SIXTEEN

Fletcher

"DANCE?" he murmured into her ear.

The wedding was over—or at least the ceremony was. Jim had remembered the rings. Hayley had fluffed Carrie's dress perfectly. His mom was on her third lemon drop and finally had chilled the fuck out.

The garter and bouquet had been tossed.

Cake had been consumed.

Now Sean and Carrie were draped over each other on the dance floor, the slow thump of a song resonating through the heated tent.

Twinkly lights and cool air.

Reminding him of the night before.

Of the distance and the wall, and how things had shifted afterward.

How Tammy had softened.

She'd held his hand as they'd walked out of the church, didn't shrug off his arm when he'd cautiously slid it around her at dinner—after the teasing had subsided and their entrees (along with an extra appetizer of fried cheese his mom in all her detailed glory had ordered for them) had arrived. Teasing Tammy had endured with just the barest hint of pink on her cheeks as she drawled a diffusing, "Oh, the power of young love," before turning the conversation to her parents and their penchant for PDA.

Which then Sean, Carrie, and he had picked up, teasing Fletcher's mom and dad about all of *their* PDA.

It had been light and easy, just like so many of his other interactions with Tammy.

Even though his heart had pulsed when she'd talked of young love—

Yes, he was falling hard and falling fast.

No, he didn't care.

Fried cheese had been consumed. Tammy hadn't seemed bothered in the least by the chicken Parmesan that his mom had ordered for her, nor by the teasing.

Nor by his arm.

She'd relaxed into his side, and at one point, she'd even rested her head on his shoulder.

They'd cleared a hurdle.

He wasn't entirely sure what that hurdle was. He only knew that she seemed to be unable or unwilling to push him away, and he was going to go with it.

He was going to charm the shit out of her.

He was going to keep clearing hurdles.

He was going to get her to like him so much that she wouldn't erect more walls, throw up *more* hurdles.

He was going to make it so she couldn't kick him out of her house, her heart. That this would continue to be more than a booty call, more than just physical chemistry and a couple of great orgasms. Fletcher was going to win her over.

And step one of his plan was dancing.

Now, he was a shit dancer.

But it was just one step in his plan to win Tammy.

Keep her close. Take advantage of the chemistry between them. Claim her heart.

"Come on, sweetheart," he murmured when she didn't move, probably because the song blaring through the air was critically romantic, "dance with me."

Conflict on her face. "Fletch—"

"I won't step on your toes, I promise," he told her, nipping lightly at her ear, hoping that he could keep that promise.

"It's not that," she said, turning her head slightly, as though offering her mouth to him.

He took that offering, slanting his mouth over hers. The kiss quickly escalated, as was typical when any part of him was touching any part of her.

But he did manage to summon some control and pull back.

Fletch extended a hand, tugged her to her feet when she dropped her palm into his.

She winced.

He froze. "What's wrong?"

"It's nothing." She started to take a step toward the dance floor.

Catching her around the waist and stepping up so his front was to her back, her perfect ass pressed to his pelvis, reminding him that it had been more than twenty-four hours since he'd had her, and as much as he'd liked holding her as they slept last night, it wasn't the same as being inside her. She'd been tipsy and sleepy and had crashed nearly the moment her head had hit the pillow—which meant he'd been able to cuddle up without her reverting to distance. A victory in and of itself, but obviously that couldn't compare with being inside her, with the passion and the heat, the way she looked at him when he was sliding home.

Because that's what it felt like.

Finding home.

The cuddling was...just another piece of the puzzle.

A big one. Or maybe a corner piece—the beginning of two directions, the building blocks for something bigger.

And *that* was enough time in his head.

He needed to focus on the present, on why Tammy was grimacing.

"What's wrong?" he asked again. "Why are you wincing?"

She took a step toward the floor, trying to pull away from him, but he kept close, continuing to enjoy the feel of her body pressed to his. "I'm fine," she muttered.

"That's not what I asked," he replied, shifting a little nearer, bringing his mouth to her ear again.

He was slowly finding all her spots—or quickly, he supposed considering he was on day three of being in a fake relationship and able to touch her, and slightly more than twenty-four hours of being in whatever type of strange in-between limbo they were currently residing within. Regardless of the timeline, her neck was sensitive, her jaw even more so. But the spot that had her melting against him every single time?

The delicate patch of skin just behind her ear.

As it did in that instant.

"Why, sweetheart?" he murmured, brushing a kiss to that spot.

A sigh, her body melting against his. "Stubborn," she muttered, but gave it up. "It's nothing. My feet are killing me, that's all. These shoes"—he flicked out his tongue, tasted her again, made her melt even more against him—"look sexy, but they're hell on my tootsies."

He smiled against her skin. "Tootsies?"

"Yup. Toot—*oh!*"

He'd scooped her up in his arms, careful to make sure the

skirt of her dress didn't lift or slip to the side and flash everyone. Because her squeal had garnered attention.

"What are you—?"

"Saving your feet," he said, carrying her toward one of the open sides of the tent.

"Oh, and are we going to dance like this, too?" she deadpanned.

He kissed the tip of her nose, smiled at the sparks in her pretty brown eyes. "Do you want to?"

She shuddered. "God no."

"Good." He stepped out of the tent, and as he took off for one of the tables that was clustered under an outdoor heater, the output of which was barely cutting through the night air—and long since abandoned as people sought the warmth of the tent— Fletch heard his brother quip, "I'm supposed to be the one doing the threshold carrying."

Fletch spun and shifted enough to raise a hand, lifting his middle finger.

Sean just laughed before returning his focus to his bride.

Fletcher didn't waste any more time or energy. He just kept walking, heading for that cluster of tables, setting Tammy down in one of the chairs. She shivered, and he draped his suit jacket over her shoulders, shifting around her to button the fabric over her front. It dwarfed her and for the first time, he realized how small she was.

Strange.

Her personality. Her *heart* always made her seem larger than life.

But she was tiny.

"You're like an adorable elf," he told her. "All you're missing are the pointy ears and the *Lord of the Rings* robes."

A roll of her eyes as she shoved her hands into the pocket of his jacket. "I'll have you know that most of the *LOTR* elves are tall."

"Really?" he asked, shifting to kneel at her feet. "How do you know that?"

"I don't." Said with such confidence that it took a beat for him to process the words. Then he burst out laughing, a longer pause as he struggled to control himself. Then, "But I choose to believe that elves are tall and slender. Thus"—her chin lifted—"they are everything I'm not."

"Well, good thing I like short and curvy."

She smiled even as she shook her head.

He reached for her ankle, started to undo the strap on her shoe.

Tammy yanked her foot away. "Wh-what are you doing?"

"Your feet hurt."

"I—"

He calmly grasped her ankle and unbuckled her shoe, slipped it off her foot. Not thinking, he leaned in and pressed a kiss to the sole of her foot.

"Fletch!" she gasped, trying to tug it back. "That's disgusting. They're probably all sweaty and—"

He held tight and kissed her toes. "Mmm," he hummed, "smells like peaches and cream."

She sputtered, asked, completely aghast. "Peaches and cream?"

"Yup." Not really. They did smell a little fruity, like the lotion he'd watched her spread over her skin that morning in the bedroom before they'd pulled on their clothes—him jeans and a tee, getting ready to meet his brother for all the groom things, her sweatpants and a purple sweater, her dress on a hanger that also had a toiletry bag hung over its hook. She'd been commandeered to go to the church and decorate with his mom before they'd met up with Carrie and Hayley. "Your skin is delicious, no matter the part."

More sputtering. "That's—"

"How did you get my mom to leave the decorating to you?"

Her mouth dropped open. "I—how did—?"

"How did I know that you somehow got my mom to relax before the lemon drops?"

Her nose wrinkled. "Yes. *That.*"

Tartness in her tone.

"I heard her telling my dad about it," he told her, reaching for her other shoe, starting to tug open the buckle, slide out the strap. "Just so you know, she's baking you *all* the things once the wedding weekend is over. Be prepared for a huge delivery, and she won't scrimp on the sugar."

A shrug. "I love sweet things."

He'd already noted that, along with her obsession with fried cheese, but since it was important enough for her to reveal to him, it was important enough for him to underline that note in his mind. "You'll probably go into a sugar coma."

"I'm fine with that." He chuckled and bent to kiss her other foot, her toes. She didn't squirm this time, but she didn't exactly look thrilled for his mouth to be down there. Also, good to note: no foot fetish.

"What's your favorite treat?" he asked, skimming his fingers along her feet.

She scowled at his movements, but since she'd stopped fighting his hold, Fletcher considered that to be a victory.

"Chocolate? Fruity?" he asked.

Her lips pressed flat, released, and he felt her relenting, especially when she said, "An easier question to answer might be what *don't* I like?"

He began massaging her feet, and *that* she liked if her

slumping back into her chair, her lids sliding closed was any indication. "What don't you like, sweetheart?" he pressed.

"Coconut," she breathed, her eyes sliding closed.

"No piña coladas?"

She waved a hand, eyes still shut. "Alcohol is a separate category from sweets." Fletcher disagreed with that statement, and if he didn't want Tammy relaxed and soft above him, he might have argued, just to watch the bright red flush of annoyance spread on her cheeks, to see her eyes spark with irritation.

But she was relaxed.

Soft.

Sweet.

Gentle.

And he wanted her to stay that way, so he continued massaging, asked, "No macaroons then?"

A flutter of her eyes, and she shook her head. "Somehow I'm not surprised that you know that I don't like macaroons and that it's macaroons that have coconut and not macarons."

He kept his voice light. "I'm a man of many talents."

She snorted, but her mouth was curved. "So long as those talents continue to be administered on my feet, I'm not going to argue with that."

With that bit of sass, he couldn't resist pushing her buttons, at least a little bit. "Next time I make macarons I'll be sure to whisk the eggs with your toes."

"First, ew." Tammy's nose wrinkled, even though she didn't open her eyes. "Second, that seems impossible. I've watched *Great British Bake-Off.* I know how much elbow grease it takes to get enough air into those egg whites." He snorted. "Third, how do you know how to make macarons?"

"I watch *Great British Bake-Off.*" A dry statement that had her eyes slitting open and glaring down at him. He added, "Despite the Lunchable lunches, my mom actually *did* cook a lot when we were growing up. In fact, she cooked and baked all the time. Used to run a little bakery and restaurant in town when we were growing up." He shifted slightly, began massaging her calves. "We learned how to bake a lot of things just by hanging out."

"Like what?" Tammy asked, flexing her toes.

It drew his gaze, and he actually looked at her feet for the first time, not just the oblique glances to see where his hands were, to see her toes distinguished from the sole and the heel. He saw her pink polish, the tiny freckle on the top of her right big toe. He saw that there were freckles in a pattern all along the top. Including beneath—

He took his hands from her legs and gripped that right foot, brushed a deep red groove that marred that delicate patten of freckles.

"What the fuck?" he whispered.

Tammy jerked slightly and he managed to tear his eyes from her injured foot to meet her stare. "What?" she asked, brows drawn tightly together.

He glanced back down at her feet.

"Wh—" she started to say again, then, "Oh." A sigh. "It's stupid," she said. "Like I said, these shoes are the devil. They're gorgeous but abuse the hell out of my feet every time I wear them."

He didn't think.

Just grabbed both shoes, stood, and walked over to a trash can, launching them into the depths of wedding waste.

"Wh-what the fuck, Fletcher?"

He leaned in, pushed her gently back into the chair when she started to stand, gripped her chin, and promptly lost his temper. "Never again will you be so casual about taking abuse, even from yourself."

She swatted his hand away, shoved him back. "Fuck off,

King. I can do whatever I want." She hopped to her feet. "If I want to abuse myself, my feet, my body or heart or mind, that's my prerogative."

A curl of fury slid through him. "No."

Her brows lifted. "*No?*"

It was a dangerous question. Well, not the word itself, but the tone she used when she expressed it. *So* fucking dangerous. Answer wrong, and he'd be screwed.

But...fuck it.

She could be pissed at him all she wanted. There was no way he could back down from this.

She'd hurt herself. For a pair of fucking shoes.

A pair of shoes she was currently trying to retrieve from the trash can, walking across the ground—where she could step on a stick or a piece of glass or a burning cigarette or...or *something* that might hurt her, however improbable—and reaching into the can.

Then nearly toppling *into* the can.

Fucking hell.

The woman needed a keeper.

Yes, that was caveman. Yes, that was stupid as hell. No, he didn't give a fuck at that particular moment in time.

He marched across the clearing, scooped her up, and carried her back to the table. "Stay," he muttered, plunking her into the chair.

"St-stay—" she stammered, steam all but flying out of her ears, her gaze so intense, he might as well have been skewered with lasers. He plunked a hand on her shoulder to keep her in place, held her there for a moment, and then he straightened, released her, knowing that she probably wouldn't stay in that chair—hell, he *knew* there was no way she'd stay in that chair.

He just needed a head start.

And he had it, making it to the trash can first.

Scooping up the shoes first.

Launching those shoes into the dark forest surrounding them...first.

Okay, he couldn't reasonably say that she'd been planning on launching the shoes into the forest.

But he still got there first.

And off they went.

They both watched them sail off amongst the needle-lined branches.

And then...*then* Tammy turned to him, her face filled with such absolute fury that for the first time in a long time, Fletcher felt as though his life were in danger.

Or if not his life, then at the very least that his balls were in grave, *grave* danger.

SEVENTEEN

Tammy

WAS there smoke coming out of her ears?

It fucking should be.

Or maybe actual flames because she had just watched the man—watched him in a cloud of absolute fury—as he threw her fucking expensive shoes into the goddamned forest.

One.

Then the other.

"What the fuck are you doing, King?" she growled, ready to do violence.

Like that TikTok trend, looking into the camera and mouthing, "I choose violence."

He merely turned to her and scooped her up, carrying her to the chair and plunking her ass down into it.

All over again.

More steam from her ears.

Enough flames to start a forest fire.

"Oh, is the asshole from the car ride making a reappearance?" she snapped, shoving him away. "I thought you promised

me you weren't actually *like* that. Or at least, that was the bullshit you tried to sell me on the way up here."

Fletcher straightened, towering over her, his hands clenched
at his sides. He was shaking, literally shaking, as he slowly
inhaled and exhaled.

He was pissed.

Perhaps as pissed as she was.

And that...well, probably it shouldn't have, but it did
anyway. Because the fact that he was furious had her anger
tempering, fading, softening.

Curiosity took the place of fury.

It made no sense.

But that was the truth.

"Why are *you* so upset?" she asked and instead of ice, her
question was almost gentle.

Time to turn in her feminist card.

Well, okay, she'd do that...right after she got the answer to
her question.

"You're hurting yourself," he gritted out his head turned
away, his jaw tight. The intensity in that statement surprised
her, made her forget about cards and feminism and questions
and answers. "I don't want you to be hurting."

Tammy tilted her head to the side, tried to understand why
this is so important to him. "But...why?"

He turned, and his expression was so aghast that the
remnants of her anger tamped down, slid away, poofed off into
space like fucking fairy dust or something. "*Why?*" he snapped.

"Yes," she said and stood, placed her hand over his heart.

It thundered beneath her palm, and more curiosity trickled
through her. "You're hurting yourself."

"Fletcher"—her nails dug lightly through his T-shirt—
"Why. Do. You. Care?"

"I—" His hands unclasped, one warm palm dropped over

hers, dwarfing her hand, the roughened skin of his callouses having her wonder once again where he'd earned them. "I care, sweetheart. You maybe don't want to hear that I do. Maybe it'll scare you and make you run. Maybe I intended to charm the fuck out of you so you wouldn't want to kick me to the curb when the weekend is done, that maybe you'd keep me when you don't keep anyone else—"

"Fletch—"

"I like you, Tammy. I know this is supposed to be pretend, but if I'm being honest with you, it's *never* just been pretend." Her throat tightened, heart pounding, pulse throbbing in her veins. "I've liked you from that first day in the office, and I like you now even more. You're smart. You're gorgeous. But more than anything else, you have a huge, kind heart."

Why did his words affect her so much?

They were just words, and she knew that words couldn't be trusted, not when there weren't actions to back them up.

But...hadn't he given her the action?

The realization had her feeling tingly from toes to top, her heart beating so hard in her chest that it felt like she was going to pass out.

Why did his words affect her so intensely?

Because they were everything she had ever wanted to hear, to believe in, and the way he was staring at her, the earnestness of his tone, the way his heart was pounding just as hard as hers was, just beneath her palm, made her believe in him.

Believe those words were more than just a talking point.

Believe they were more than some line of bullshit he was giving her when he intended to fuck her over later—fuck her over like Calvin—

No.

She blinked, and pulled away, turning her back on him as the memories sliced right through her.

Cold. She was so fucking cold in an instant.

Her feet suddenly felt frozen, soaking up the frosty ground. Her heart was a block of ice and—

No.

She couldn't think about Calvin, about how it had changed everything. About—

"I'm not worth it, Fletch." The words flew out of her, sharp painful slices on the way up her throat, over her tongue. "I'm messed up inside. I'll never be a woman who can—"

"You can." No hesitation. No room in his tone for negotiation.

She froze. "I—"

Fingers on her jaw. "You. *Can.* You're scared. I don't know why, and I don't know that I care." She choked as those fingers traced down her neck. "I want to know if and when you're ready to tell me. I want to know what is making your eyes fill with shadows, what makes you think that you're messed up and not worth it. But I don't care." His fingers closed lightly over her throat. "I don't care about those fucked up thoughts, the painful memories. Because knowing them won't change one damned thing about the way I feel about you."

"Stop talking," she whispered.

"Because they're bullshit. Those thoughts are bullshit. Because you *are* worth it. You aren't messed up—not any more than any other human on this planet." A gentle squeeze, drawing her gaze to his when all she wanted to do was allow it to flit off into the distance, to remain unfocused and distant, to not let the words affect her.

But they had already affected her.

They added a layer, a *thousand* layers to that bubble of protection he'd erected the night before.

"You have to stop talking," she said softly.

Begged.

"You can tell me on your own terms," he said, ignoring her, still talking, each of those words colliding with her, filling her up in a way that she'd never experienced before. Because this man made her feel things she shouldn't. Because he was stubborn and pushy and...he liked her, even with the chip on her shoulder, with all the barbed wire and concrete that was her attempt to keep him, to keep everyone safely at a distance.

"You have to st—"

Another squeeze, this time accompanied by the "I won't push you for answers," he went on. "And yes, I fucking want to hear all the things that make you, *you*. But I won't sugarcoat it, babe. Whatever—*who*ever—made you feel like shit is a fucking idiot, and nothing you tell me will convince me otherwise." He released her. "Because I've seen the woman you are inside, and you are *incredible*."

Finally, it was too much.

"Fuck," she whispered, stepping away from him, her hands going to her hair, panic slicing through her.

Run.

Run.

Run.

A gentle hand on her shoulder.

"No, Tammy," Fletcher said softly. "Stay, honey," he murmured, and she realized with a start that she'd spoken aloud. "Stay and reach for what you deserve. Even if that's not me. Even if it's not a relationship or a boyfriend or *more*. Stay and grab on to someone who sees you for the wonderful person you are in here." He tapped her chest, just above where her heart thundered below.

"I'm..."

Scared.

Terrified.

Torn to shreds and pieced back together.

But not by Fletcher. Who got furious when she hurt her feet just because she wore uncomfortable shoes. Who encouraged her to find someone who saw her as wonderful.

Wonderful!

Fletcher, who thought she was worth it.

And...why should he be the only one who thought she was worth it? Why shouldn't she look inside and see herself as worthy? Maybe she didn't want to be in a relationship, but that should be born of preference and choice and not of a fear of getting too close.

It shouldn't be because of Calvin.

Of the way he'd left her with no choice but to erect those walls.

No. That wasn't fair. He hadn't been the only cause. She'd fallen into that trap because it was easier to keep out than to let in, because, yeah, Calvin had hurt her. But lots of people got hurt, and it was her own pain and insecurity that made it safer to just keep her distance.

Heat at her spine.

But Fletcher didn't touch her.

Just stood near enough to let her know he was there.

And that closeness made the words come. Not the deepest, most buried truth. Not everything about Calvin, not yet. She had to unpack that in her own brain first. But the rest of it. The pain that she'd shared with her siblings, her parents.

"My mom had cancer."

Now his hands came to her, his arms wrapping around her, his body coming flush against her back. "I'm sorry."

"She's better now," Tammy whispered. "Has been in remission for years."

"That still leaves a mark."

She nodded. "I'm the baby. Barely old enough to remember

her in the hospital, but even though I was the baby, I remember in other ways."

He waited as she gathered her thoughts, just holding her tightly, securely.

Protectively.

And the words came again.

"It was silly. She was—*is*—the glue that holds us together. Always at every school event, driving us to sports, asking us about our day at dinner. All the typical Mom stuff."

"And that changed when she was sick?"

"My dad is amazing. He tried to pick up the slack, and we had great family friends and neighbors who stepped in. It was just...with four kids and one parent missing, others trying to pick up the slack...things got forgotten." A beat. "Understandably," she added quickly, feeling guilty for even bringing this up. "It's stupid," she hissed. "It's not important—"

"Except it *is*," he countered. "What happened, love?"

"I got forgotten."

A long pause. "What do you mean?"

"I mean there were four kids in our family. We all played sports or were in school clubs or had playdates with friends, and...it was a lot to keep track of."

His fingers spasmed, digging into her torso for a second before gentling. "You were forgotten." His voice had gone a little rough. "How often, sweetheart?"

The music inside the tent changed, an upbeat song blaring through the speakers and Tammy finally remembered where they were at, what they should—and shouldn't—be doing. "We should go back inside," she said. "You're missing your brother's—"

"Carrie already told me that she's going to dance until her feet fall off—"

"Don't have a problem with her wearing uncomfortable shoes, do you?" she asked, trying to change the subject.

He brought it right back to her. "Carrie's not you, is she?"

Tammy sucked in a breath.

Fletcher turned her in his arms, cupping her jaw and tilting her head up. "No," he said. "I can answer that one for you. She's *not* you. Not by a long shot."

"And Trina?" she asked. "You care about her. You—" She cut herself off.

He went still, his hand flexing on her face. "Some part of me will always care about her."

Why had she brought Trina up? Probably because Tammy had seen the other woman, the beautiful other woman who'd introduced herself to Tammy and been nice—fucking *nice!* Tammy hated the woman for hurting Fletcher, wanted her to be a mean troll who sniffed at her and treated everyone with disdain.

But Trina was nice.

As was Trina's mom.

She saw why Connie had found it difficult to let them go.

Hell, Trina had brought her a plate of appetizers when Tammy had missed the chance at them because she'd packed up decorations at the church—not wanting Connie and Tony to have to worry about it that night, especially when they were taking family pictures, and especially not wanting them to have to get up early like Connie had told her she was planning on doing.

And then after Tammy had downed the plate—more fried cheese and delicious stuffed meatballs and a piece of cantaloupe that had the serving of food masquerading as something sort of healthy—Trina had fixed her hair and nudged her toward Fletcher, telling her that she would finish up so that Tammy could enjoy the rest of her night.

Trina had brought her food and fixed her hair!

What the actual fuck of a universe had she stumbled upon?

Fletcher's ex was as nice as he was.

And it was a good thing that Trina had fixed Tammy's hair because Tammy *had* ended up in some of the family pictures.

Fake relationship to family pictures.

Insanity.

Tammy released a breath. "Trina seems really nice," she whispered. "I want to hate her for hurting you, but..."

"She *is* nice," he admitted. "I mean, it would be nicer if she hadn't gotten married to someone else so quickly." He huffed out a laugh. "Her finding someone she saw as husband material so soon after we broke up was hell on the ego."

Tammy winced. "I'm—"

"But the truth is that even though it took me a bit to get over her, I can see that she made the right decision in ending our relationship. We..." A sigh. "We wouldn't have made each other happy. Not in the long term."

"I'm sure it still sucked."

He slid his hand into her hair. "So did yours." He brushed his lips over hers. "Should we talk more about how much our past traumas sucked? Or should I tell you that after Carrie's feet fall off, she's apparently taking my brother back to their place so she can ride him like a show pony."

Tammy froze. "You're kidding."

A shudder wracked his strong, muscular frame. "I wish I was," he muttered. "I don't know why Carrie insists on telling me these things."

"Because she sees herself as your sister and likes to torture you?"

A shrug. "Probably."

She laughed.

He did too, for just a moment. Then his face went serious

again and she stiffened, lungs stilling, pulse picking up again. "I know that's not everything," he whispered. "I know that's not the only reason you're good at keeping your distance."

Tammy sucked in a breath, battened down the hatches.

And it was a good thing she braced herself.

Because his next words shook her to the core.

"But know this," he said, "I won't forget you, Tammy."

"Fletcher," she whispered.

"You're imprinted on my heart and soul." Another brush of his lips over hers. "And you're staying there."

Her breath caught. Her eyes stung. She opened her mouth to say...

Something.

Then the DJ's voice came onto the speakers scattered through the tent. "Join me for saying goodbye to the newest Mr. and Mrs. King!"

"So much for her feet falling off," Fletcher muttered. "I guess show pony time has—"

"Come on!" Tammy hissed. "We can't miss waving them off!" Reaching for his hand, she snagged it and then dragged him forward, her bare feet flying over the ground for all of two steps before Fletcher swept her up into his arms again, carrying her toward the tent.

They reached the tent's exit, and Fletcher set her onto her feet just as Carrie and Sean were being cheered off, huge smiles and loving expressions on their faces.

She and Fletcher yelled and threw confetti made out of dried leaves.

They clapped and shouted as the car with its Just Married sign taped to the back windshield, cans dragging and making a ton of noise, streamers flying in the wind pulled away.

She sniffed—fucking weddings.

Fletcher wiped her cheeks, dashing away her tears, and then

he bent and murmured in her ear, "What's the likelihood that *you'll* ride me like a show pony tonight?"

Shock had her mouth dropping open.

But only for a second.

Because then amusement boiled up and over, and she found herself laughing hysterically, laughing so hard that she had to brace her hands on her knees as she tried to catch her breath.

"Is that a no?" he asked, crouching in front of her, covering her hands with his own.

Suddenly, her laughter faded.

Need took its place.

She wanted this man and his protective words, the promise of not forgetting. She wanted the bossy and annoying and the funny man who made her laugh.

But she was Tammy Fucking Huntington.

So, she had to throw some sass, some fire his way.

Slowly, she straightened and plunked her hands on her waist.

"You find me some more of that fried cheese, and I'll ride you any which way you want."

EIGHTEEN

Fletcher

THE SCENT of fall in his nose.

A curvy body pressed to his.

Tammy.

He knew before he was even fully awake, knew there would be no thinking that Tammy was Trina. Not ever again.

And somehow, he was awake before Tammy.

Probably because they'd done all sorts of riding when they'd gotten back to the house last night—show pony and wild monkey sex, against the wall and on the dresser and when they'd gone to clean up, in the shower, too.

He was wiped.

She'd barely stayed awake long enough to make it to the bed. Her eyes had already been sliding closed, even before she'd made it under the covers.

And she was still out.

But he wasn't.

Weird.

He settled back down into the mattress, started to close his eyes again...and then he heard it. Heard what must have drawn him out of deep sleep, something his body had been trained to listen for because it had happened so many times over the years.

A pebble on his window.

The scratch of a branch on the glass.

Trina.

He sat up with a start, dislodging Tammy from his chest, but she was so out of it that she didn't even move. Slowly, he shifted, pulling back the covers, and sliding from the bed. Trina *was* there, scratching his windowpane with a long branch they kept hidden beneath the back porch. It was early. So early that the horizon to the west was barely beginning to lighten.

She scratched again, and he yanked open the pane.

Then nearly got impaled by the end of the stick.

He dodged, snagged the end. "Trina," he hissed, trying not to wake Tammy. "What the fuck are you doing?"

"Come down," she called.

He shook his head. "No, Tri, I'm—"

"Just come down," she said. "It's important." Her voice was too loud. She was going to wake Tammy up, and then that was going to be a very awkward conversation—having to explain why his married ex was making a pre-dawn call to the house, summoning him like she was Romeo and he was Juliet.

"Okay," he said. "Just"—he held up a hand—"just *okay.* Give me a second."

Quietly, he slid the frame closed then picked his way across the room, searching the shadows for any obstacles that might make him eat shit. And there were plenty of them. He and Tammy hadn't exactly been neat the night before, and there were shoes and belts and jackets and underwear scattered to and fro.

And seriously, *fro?*

Apparently, he sounded like a fictional fairy godmother at zero dark thirty in the morning.

Snorting inwardly, he yanked up a pair of sweats, shrugged into a hoodie, and tugged on his socks and boots. Then made his way quietly from the room, down the stairs, and out onto the back deck.

Trina was leaning against the railing, her hair piled on top of her head.

He used to love when she wore her hair that way, loved to go up behind her and kiss the back of her neck, to do his level best to mess up that pile of hair, to send it tumbling down, to send *her* tumbling down onto any semi-flat surface around.

Today, he found he wasn't drawn to her.

Yes, she was effortlessly beautiful.

Yes, they'd once had chemistry.

But he wasn't pining to get back with her. There was affection. There always would be, but he meant what he'd said the night before.

He and Trina were over.

A happy memory, but just that. A memory.

One he'd clung to for far too long.

One that paled in the face of what he had with Tammy.

"Hey," Trina said, pushing off the railing and moving toward him. She hugged him tightly, and he was struck by how wrong it felt to have her body pressed to his.

"Hey," he said, releasing her.

She hopped up on the railing.

He hopped up next to her, watching as her feet swung back and forth. She was quiet for long enough that he began to wonder if she were actually going to speak at all, but he didn't press her. Trina always needed time to ponder, to pull together her thoughts.

She couldn't be pushed.

It would make her feel panicked, the words stoppering up in the back of her throat, and then he'd have to spend even more time waiting for her to try to gather what she'd wanted to say.

Such a frustrating habit.

He understood it, of course. Everyone had their things. But it was just really nice that Tammy didn't have that problem.

"I was jealous when I saw her at the wedding."

Fletcher inhaled sharply through his nose. "Trina." A warning to not go down this path. It was dead and gone, put to rest. He wanted to continue to look back on their time together as having some positives, and if she went down the path he was thinking she was going to go, this was quickly going to turn into a shitshow.

"She gorgeous," Trina said. "And you've always had that thing for redheads." She turned her head and grinned at him. He felt some of the tension fade. That was mischief in her eyes, in the curve of her lips.

"I have," he agreed.

More quiet, and he found himself staring up at the sky and the fading stars, their light dimming as the sun rose higher in the sky.

"We've needed to have this conversation for a while," she said softly.

"You mean discussing my fondness for redheads?"

She swatted his arm then rested her head on his shoulder. Even that didn't feel right. Because she wasn't Tammy. Because it wasn't red hair tickling his neck. Because it wasn't Tammy's scent in his nose. "You know I mean about us."

"There is no *us*."

She lifted her head. "Don't say that."

Fear churned through his body, and Fletch began to wonder if he'd seriously misjudged this situation so badly.

Her hand rested on his cheek. "Don't say that," she repeated.

"Trina." Another warning.

"There will always be an *us*."

Fuck.

He inhaled again.

"You're a part of my past," she whispered. "And that will always tie us together."

His breath sliced out of him, but she kept talking.

"That, we can't change. We have too much history—I remember the time you got lost on Steep Locket Ridge. I know that you prefer your pizza without cheese. We were each other's first kiss, first time, practically our first *everything*." She sighed. "But that doesn't mean we would have been happy."

"I know," he said cautiously. "That's why we broke up, remember?"

Soft, tinkling laughter. "I remember, and maybe I'm coming here at the wrong time, saying all the wrong things, but I stayed awake all night thinking of you."

He smothered a wince. "Trina, that's not—"

"Thinking that I'm so glad you found someone who looks at you right."

He went stiff, nearly toppled himself off the railing.

"She busted her ass during that wedding, Fletch. She was everywhere, making sure a woman she'd met only this weekend had as gorgeous of a wedding as she'd ever dreamed of. Tammy packed up the church so your parents didn't have to. She helped the florist when all the centerpieces toppled over as the florist was wheeling them in, helping to put them back together so that they looked perfect. Hayley's hem tore? She found a sewing kit and sorted it. Your Aunt Becky was getting a little sloppy after enjoying too many lemon drops? She brought her glasses of water like it was her job. She"—Trina stopped and shook her head—"was amazing."

"She *is* amazing."

"I know." Trina sighed. "And it's not fair that I felt jealous, that I still feel possessive of you. God knows I've moved on."

He snorted.

She punched him. "Even though I was feeling a bit jealous and possessive, it wasn't in the normal way. Or maybe it was. I was feeling...protective." A sigh. "I didn't want you to be hurt—which isn't fair, I know, because I'm the one who ended us and did it in a spectacularly immature way—not talking to you, pretending it was all going to be fine, that we would be fine, and it would all just work out because we'd been together for so long, because I love your parents as much as my own."

"It's not like that," he said, grabbing her hand and squeezing it lightly. "Now I see it as brave. You did what needed to be done, did it when I couldn't. Because"—another squeeze—"I was too scared to admit that we weren't going to work out."

Her expression softened. "It was...I miss you. I love you. I know I did the right thing, of course. For both of us, but part of me still misses us, you know?"

He tugged a lock of her hair. "I know."

"But yeah, I also know that even though I miss you and miss *us*, when I heard you were bringing someone, I didn't know if this woman was going to treat you—my special, amazing first *everything*—right."

His heart squeezed. "Trina."

"So, I know I hurt you, hurt both of us. I know I should have talked to you way before the rehearsal dinner, but I was so scared to ruin us. I know I've apologized before, but I really am sorry for waiting until then and for blurting it out the way I did—"

"I'm not." A beat, her shocked eyes coming to his. "Did I

feel blindsided? Yes. Did I get my heart broken? Also, yes. Did it fucking hurt to see you moving on so quickly when I felt rocked to the core? Yeah, honey, it did." She winced, and he nudged her shoulder. "But then I let all of that go and realized that you'd done the right thing, that maybe we would have been happy together, stayed together, but we wouldn't have *more*."

She nudged him back. "More is pretty great, isn't it?"

Fletcher smiled. "*So* now are you going to stop apologizing for five minutes and tell me why you're really here?"

A frown. "Brute." Another wince. "No. That was me."

"Truly, I'm not sorry you hurt me," he said softly. "It sucked for sure. But Trin, it worked out for the better for both of us."

"Of course, you're not sorry. Not now," she quipped, "that you have an awesome Tammy who stares at you like you hung the moon, and you care enough about her that you're launching expensive Jimmy Choo's into the woods."

"You—" He winced. Of course, someone had seen. There had been more than a hundred people in that tent, in those woods.

"Hubs and I snuck out for a bit," she said softly. "And when we were sneaking back in, we stumbled on you two arguing. About shoes." Her lips quirked.

He winced again. "I was an ass."

A smirk. "You were." She patted his cheek. "But you never were that much of an ass with *me*." Another pat. "You never cared that my feet pinched, that I might have pushed myself too far, or that I planned on eating an entire carton of ice cream and was going to regret it later."

"I'm not dumb enough to come between you and your ice cream."

A roll of her eyes. "Dork."

"And proud."

Smiling as she dropped her hand, she said, "I'd wager that if she was going to eat it all, knowing full well she was lactose intolerant and would be in agony later, you'd launch the carton of ice cream into the woods to rest with the fishes alongside her shoes."

Since that was true, he just nodded.

"You found her, honey. You found the woman you're meant to be with, and I love you enough that it makes me so damned happy." She hugged him tight. "And I love you enough that I had to tell you that."

A flicker of movement around the corner of the house.

He glanced up to see Trina's husband appear. "Dom is here?"

"He drove me." She straightened and smiled at her husband, who nodded and leaned against the corner of the house, waiting for her to finish talking to her ex, after driving his wife to her ex's house really fucking early in the morning.

Dom was *her* more.

"I'm glad you found him, too," he murmured, tilting his chin toward Dom.

Her face went gentle, so damned gentle that his throat went tight, his eyes burned.

"I think he'd take your ice cream," he said, forcing out the words, going for teasing because it was either that or he'd start bawling, and as much as he still cared about Trina, still loved her, he'd much rather be up in bed with Tammy than freezing his ass off crying on the porch with his ex.

"He would." A beat. "He has."

Fletcher laughed, shaking his head as he jumped down from the railing, helped her down. Then he hugged her, told her goodbye, and shoved her in the direction of her husband.

Turned to go back to who was important.

Tammy.

He bounded up the stairs, pushed open the door to the bedroom, and...

Stopped dead.

Tammy was out of bed.

Standing by the window.

Looking *out* the window.

NINETEEN

Tammy

FLETCHER'S FACE TIGHTENED.

With guilt?

That certainly would have been more convenient because her insides were churning like she'd been dropped into a blender. Apple slices and frozen pieces of banana and ice cubes all flying toward those blades, spinning and being chopped up smaller and smaller and *smaller* until they were transformed into liquid.

Her heartbeat was loud, too.

Echoing in her ears, roaring like those blades did when they met the chunks of fruit.

But it wasn't guilt.

It was remorse, and based on the very sweet conversation she'd eavesdropped on—yeah, yeah, she shouldn't have invaded his privacy. No, she couldn't find herself regretting it, not when he looked like this.

Not when he was worried he'd hurt her.

Not when he crossed to her, took her hands in his, and said, "It's not what you think."

"That's what someone guilty would say."

His fingers convulsed. "Tammy—"

She squeezed his hands back, knew that what she felt for him meant that she couldn't run from the swirling terror in her, just like she couldn't allow him to feel bad, not because he was worried about her.

This was shoes launched into a forest.

This was a protective bubble she wanted to erect over *him*.

Because it did something to her to see him hurting, to see him in pain.

"I heard you get up," she admitted, "and I know I shouldn't have been doing it, but I eavesdropped." A quiet breath. "I heard everything."

"Everything?"

She nodded. The entire conversation had reinforced what Tammy had thought of Trina at the wedding—a good woman. One it would have been easy for her to hate, if she wasn't so damned nice. And brave, to risk the happiness of both their families so that she and Fletcher could both find something that meant more.

Something Tammy was starting to understand the meaning of.

Because the fake part of her relationship with him had lasted all of a couple of hours. Fake had gone out the window the moment her lips touched his. It had fucking flown into space the moment she'd realized how much it hurt when he'd called her Trina in bed because even though she'd had all of a couple of hours with the man, she'd been feeling so much more with Fletcher than she'd ever felt before, even with Calvin.

The man she'd once had so many dreams with.

The man who'd nearly destroyed who she was as a person.

The man who'd made her feel more than forgotten, more than she'd *ever* felt as a child, as a teenager, a young woman lost in the shuffle of a big family.

"We're good," she said. "I—" The protective bubble around him hardened, stiffened until she was encasing him in concrete and barbed wire and steel. "I heard it all—what she said, what you said. I'm fine, and..." She swallowed hard. Why was it so hard to say this? To open herself up? Okay, fucking fine, she *knew* why it was so hard. It was the wasteland she'd been living in since Calvin had fucking napalmed her life. "It's good. I'm good. *We're* good."

"I don't want our good to include any fakeness."

She laughed shakily. "I'm pretty sure that all the fakeness ended the moment I kissed you."

He stepped a little closer. "I'm pretty sure any fakeness was on your side, baby."

Whirling.

Terror.

Then his arms wrapped around her, and that bubble tightened, sliding closer, slipping under the spinning blades, covering her, protecting her.

She could breathe and think and *love*.

Love.

In one weekend.

Now *that* made her want to run straight into the bathroom and slam the door...and text *herself* a breakup message.

Maybe that made her a bad girlfriend.

Girlfriend.

She breathed, dodged the blades, embraced the bubble, and thought that maybe it made her a *great* one that she could finally think the word.

And maybe, say it aloud.

"No fake," she agreed and she fucking leaped past those

blades and went for it. "Just a woman embracing her inner girlfriend."

His face lit. "Yeah?"

She shoved his shoulder. "That's what I said, isn't it?"

He stepped close, cupped her cheek. "Yeah, honey, that's what you said."

She opened her mouth, readying herself to snark back, but the words didn't even get a chance to tinge the air with joyful sarcasm—*ha*—because Fletcher shoved her hard. She squeaked, arms flailing, her stomach dropping, and then...

Her back collided gently with the mattress.

Fletcher came down on top of her. "Thank you," he said, cupping her cheek. "And you need to know that I'm not going fuck it up."

That made her heart squeeze, her fear transform into a gas, somehow drifting in through tiny imperfections in her walls, sliding through her bubble, invading her nose, her eyes, her mouth.

Because she wasn't worried about Fletcher fucking things up.

She was worried she would.

In fact, with her track record, it was almost certain that she *would*.

TWENTY

Fletcher

MONDAY MORNING COFFEE WAS KEY.

Only this was the first time he was pouring coffee into two mugs, adding cream and sugar to his own, but not to Tammy's.

Because she apparently took her coffee like a *man*.

Laughing to himself, he thought of how she'd teased him after they'd managed to pry themselves from the bed, had stumbled down for sustenance and caffeine to hold them over until the post-wedding brunch. So much fire in Tammy Huntington, and he kind of loved it.

No, he *did* love it.

Four days together, and he was gone for this girl.

Of course, he'd admired her for much longer, had spent a lot of timing building a friendship with the crumbs she kept throwing his way. So, a lot more had happened than he'd been expecting this weekend, and he'd ended up with a hell of a lot more than crumbs from Tammy.

A girlfriend.

He'd ended up with a girlfriend.

So, all in all, he couldn't complain.

Hell, he could barely contain his smile. Complaining wasn't anywhere on his radar.

"Thanks, baby," she said softly when he set the mug on the desk of her office. He knew that she had a call in just a couple of minutes so just squeezed her hand and headed out. He knew that because she'd brought him coffee barely an hour before—with his cream and sugar—and had told him she had back-to-back meetings straight through lunch and all the way to the end of the day.

Missing Friday meant a bit more work than normal for him, though not back-to-back meetings all day.

So, he left her to it, was smiling when he heard her dialing into the call before he quietly shut the door, even as he made plans to order lunch for her. Maybe he'd put a note inside, see if he could talk his way into her bed that night.

Hell, he'd start throwing pebbles at the glass of *her* bedroom window, find a branch and scratch, pry it open and crawl in Romeo-style—

Okay, maybe not the last.

That would be creepy.

The rest of it...yeah, that he'd do. In a heartbeat.

"*What* is that?"

Lisa's voice made him jump, made him realize that he'd been standing in the corridor, daydreaming about throwing rocks at a window.

What. A. Weirdo.

He blinked and tried to play dumb. "What is what?" he asked, turning toward Lisa.

Her arms were crossed, and she tilted her head toward her office. "Inside. Door closed." And then she strode forward into her office without waiting to see if he'd obey.

Which he would.

Because that was five-feet-six-inches of fire waiting to explode on his ass.

Fuck.

This had the potential to be very, very bad.

What gave you the clue to that genius? his inner asshole muttered.

Regardless, he followed Lisa in.

He'd take his licks like the sugar-and-cream-coffee-drinking man he was.

"Sit," Lisa ordered after having shut the door. "Now," she said once his ass had hit the seat of the chair in front of her desk, "please, God, tell me why you just left Tammy Huntington's office looking like you're fucking in *love*. And tell me," she went on before he could answer, "why the fuck the same Tammy Huntington brought *you* coffee, wearing that same lovey-dovey expression barely an hour ago?"

"We're dating."

Lisa's eyes went wide. "Are you fucking with me?"

"No."

Silence.

Then Lisa groaned and flopped into her chair, her head dropping back, gaze going to the ceiling. "My department," she moaned. "My department is totally fucked."

"What do you mean?" he asked genuinely confused.

"Young fucking love," she muttered. "Young fucking love fucking up my department."

Fletcher rolled his eyes. "Didn't you marry your secretary?"

She pointed a finger at him. "Don't you bring up useless information!" Another groan, but Fletcher wasn't offended. Lisa was all bark and no bite...and she'd been happily married to her ten-year-younger man for the last two decades.

"So says the HR manager," he quipped.

Her eyes narrowed. "You know that's not what we do in this part of the department."

It wasn't. That much was true.

They were under the larger umbrella of HR yes, but they didn't deal with employee complaints and conflicts, or help new hires coordinate resources. Their department was focused on diversity, and they were making real changes and doing real research in the tech industry.

"I'm just saying, you and Jon work together, and it's not an issue."

"Because he doesn't report to me," she said. "Because even though he's technically in the HR department, he's not under me. Not any longer." Her eyes met Fletcher's. "And we had to make that choice. It was either I move positions or he did."

Change jobs? What the fuck?

His brows yanked down. "But Tammy doesn't report to me."

Lisa sighed. "She's technically beneath you. You're management. She's just a human resource officer."

Tammy wasn't *just* anything.

She might be the newest member of their team, but she was one of the brightest people he'd ever worked with. Smarter than him, that was damned sure.

"You need to register your relationship with Rubil," Lisa said, "fill out the proper paperwork, and then as much as it pains me, one of you needs to transfer out of my department." Sighing, she rubbed her face. "Maybe we can put Tammy under Philip's management. Then I can still have her on a contract basis, and—"

"Wait," he said. "Just...promote her. You said she's one of your best employees. Then there wouldn't be the issue of different management levels."

Lisa rubbed her forehead. "Fletch. You've been here six

years. Tammy's barely coming up on her one-year anniversary. I can't just promote her outside of normal channels. That's not fair for anyone else in the department."

"I—"

"So, you need to decide, Fletch."

He frowned. "Decide what?"

Another sigh.

A long pause, but before he could ask her again, her office lane rang. "Decide if she's worth it, Fletch. You have to decide if Tammy is worth all the trouble you're going to bring to the team, to the important work that we're doing here." The phone rang again, and she reached for the receiver.

Her eyes locked onto his.

"You have to decide if it's worth all the trouble a relationship with her is going to bring to both of your careers."

TWENTY-ONE

Tammy

IT WAS THURSDAY NIGHT, which meant dinner and prickly pear margaritas.

Now Tammy was a girl who liked a margarita.

But the prickly pear variety was her favorite.

"What's the deal with the empty chair?" her friend Cora asked from her other side.

Probably because Tammy had been ultra-protective of the seat as their crew had tumbled in from outside the restaurant, everyone lingering in front and talking about their weeks while they'd waited for stragglers to show up. Tammy had missed last week's friends' dinner because of the wedding—something she needed to hold over Fletcher, she decided.

She'd bet with she could get him to make her his chocolate chip cookies again.

They were, perhaps, the best thing she'd ever put in her mouth, and that included the arrangement of sweet things that Connie had overnighted for her. They'd arrived in the office Tuesday morning, and though she didn't want to share once she saw the muffins and the homemade chocolate croissants and the cranberry white chocolate chip cookies, she had gone around the office and let her coworkers have some.

Some meaning one.

A single treat each.

And that was it.

Fletcher had bemoaned what he'd called the baked treat one-upmanship—even though he had quickly reached for a streusel-topped muffin, and even more quickly consumed it. That night after work, he'd showed up on her porch—like he had the evening before and the evening after, for that matter—with grocery bags in his hands. He'd made her dinner, whipped up his chocolate chip cookies, then had joked that he would crumble them over her naked body and lick them up.

She'd laughed.

He'd laughed.

Then she'd taken that joke and made it a reality.

It wasn't chocolate syrup, but his cookies were a hundred times tastier, so they'd made it work.

And made it work *good*.

Ha.

"Earth to Tammy," Cora called, and Tammy felt her cheeks heat. Not good. Cora was going to know something was up, even without the empty chair that was becoming the elephant in the room because that's what everyone kept looking at.

Kate and Jamie. Brad and Heidi. Stef and Ben. Kelsey and Tanner. And her and Cora.

The two single ladies.

They always joked they were the outcasts, the only two untethered ones. Tammy because she'd been allergic to relationships forever (a convenient lie she realized now, but one she'd clung to since her family didn't know about Calvin and how he'd shattered her into a million pieces). Cora was single because she wanted that happy ending, but had six overprotective brothers who had made it their mission to prevent their baby sister from dating anyone who wasn't worthy of her.

And, for the record, they had decided that *no* man was worth her.

So, for ages Tammy and Cora had been the only single ones at the table.

Now there was an empty chair next to Tammy, and Cora was giving her the Eye. Their coupled-up friends were all just looking somewhere on the scale of smug to all-knowing.

Cora was part of the friend group because she had always been—Kate, Kels, Heidi, and her had been friends forever (well, since college). Stef worked with Heidi and was amazing and smart, perfect for the talented, brilliant women at the table. Tammy, on the other hand, had been enveloped in because she was Brad and Jaime's sister.

Oh, she couldn't deny that the women had been great friends, and she loved them.

But she was biologically related to half of the couples at the table.

She'd had an in, and they hadn't had an easy out.

It just would be nice if...

Sigh.

If they'd picked her. Not because they were trying to be nice or wanted to please their significant others, but because they'd looked at Tammy and wanted to be her friend.

But...Fletcher had picked her.

Fake start or not, he'd made it clear he saw her, wanted her, *picked* her.

"You're dating someone!"

Tammy's eyes flew open when Kate exclaimed that loudly enough to bring down the entire restaurant, and Tammy realized she'd been sitting there fantasizing about Fletcher and all the good things he'd brought into her life instead of recognizing that she—not the chair—had become the center of attention.

God, she was acting like a dope.

Like a dope who'd just revealed everything.

As if the empty chair hadn't already revealed...what she hadn't actually announced yet. Ugh. Her inner monologue was giving her a headache.

"Look at her face. *Of course,* she's dating someone," Heidi exclaimed. "She's got lovestruck written all over her."

"And she *likes* him," Kels crooned.

Tammy got it together when Kelsey extended the *likes* to schoolyard proportions. "Kels," she snapped. "Be a grown up."

"Yeah, hell no," Kels said. "Being an adult isn't any fun. I'd rather find out about the guy who's making your cheeks turn that pretty shade of red."

"Yeah," Jaime muttered. "I'd like that, too."

Uh-oh, protective older brother alert.

"Jaim—" she began.

"Me, too," Brad said, his eyes narrowed and gleaming.

A deadly gleam.

Protective older brother times two alert.

"Uh-oh," Cora murmured, and Tammy's stomach clenched. She wasn't used to being on the receiving end of brotherly attention—hell, she wasn't sure if Fletcher was either. Maybe she should text him, tell him to abort.

They were all of a week into this.

Meeting her brothers was a terrible idea. Hell, one of them was probably already texting her mom, and then her parents would be calling her for details—chances were that they might even show up here tonight.

A risk now that they lived in town.

Oh God.

What had she gotten herself in to?

But when she'd told Fletch she wouldn't be home this evening, and had seen the disappointment on his face, she'd spontaneously invited him to this dinner with her friends. They got together every Thursday they could, the whole group of them. It was loud and fun and filled with prickly pear margaritas and tacos.

Best night of the week usually.

Now that top spot had been taken over by nights with Fletcher.

So, she'd extended the invitation and he'd surprised her by agreeing—no, that wasn't fair. Truthfully, he *hadn't* surprised her. She'd known he would agree to come.

Because he wanted to be with her.

Because he liked spending time with her.

Because she wanted him to meet her friends, for them to see...

Him picking *her*.

"I'm—"

The doors to the restaurant opened and she knew...*knew* that it was Fletcher. Was it some sixth sense she now possessed? A unique Fletcher pheromone she detected in the air?

The ball of dread in her stomach?

His gaze came to hers unerringly, and he started toward the table, eyes locked on hers, the rest of the world not existing. Just him. Just her. Just them.

And then he was there. Shoving the empty chair away, crouching down next to her, cupping her cheek with one hand. "What is it, baby?"

Her throat was filled with chalk, choking her, making her feel like she had to gasp and cough.

But then Fletcher leaned in and whispered, "Do I need to pull out the chocolate chip cookie I have stashed in my pocket?"

That chalk cleared.

Her lungs unstuck, and she felt herself go soft. "Do you really have a chocolate chip cookie in your pocket?"

He grinned and rocked back slightly on his heels, reaching into his pocket, and pulling out a zip top bag. Inside was a slightly worse for wear chocolate chip cookie. He opened the top, and she reached in and yanked out the sweet treat, shoved an insanely large bite into her mouth.

"Better?" he asked on a laugh.

She nodded.

"Now, why the panic?"

The cookie was on the way to her mouth, her lips parted and tongue flat, readying for another huge bite, but his question reminded her that they had an audience.

Cheeks heating, she turned back to the table.

Everyone was staring.

Not one of the lot of them were making any effort to hide the fact that they were openly watching her interact with Fletcher.

"I never thought of taming her with cookies," Brad quipped. "Come on man, you're shirking on your eldest brother duties. How did you miss that?"

Jaime snorted. "Did you forget about the bags of Chips Ahoy Mom used to carry around?"

Heidi smacked Brad. "Stop being obnoxious," she snapped. "Or should I talk about what I carry around to tame *you?*"

Brad flushed.

"Oh now, *this* is more interesting than Tammy being tamed with chocolate," Cora—bless her heart—said. "It's not like all of us don't know that she has a sweet tooth. Heidi, what—"

Brad covered his wife's mouth with his hand. "Don't finish that question," he said, stabbing a finger in Cora's direction. "Otherwise, I won't use my connections to get you that discount in the Maldives."

Cora glared. "I don't need your discount, Brad Huntington."

"But it's a nice perk," he countered. "Plus, I can get you upgraded to an ocean view suite."

A huff and Tammy knew he'd won. Cora's expression was murderous, but she turned the topic of the conversation to what other perks Brad could secure for her in exchange for her not pushing the topic of what had made him blush like that.

In the meantime, her brief respite in place, she turned to Fletch, eyes wide, panic no doubt written onto her face.

"What, sweetheart?"

"I forgot you coming here tonight means that you'll have to meet my brothers."

"I didn't, Tam," he said, tucking a lock of her hair behind her ear with a gentleness that made her heart squeeze. "You mentioned that your brothers are married to your friends. I knew what I was getting into."

The larger conversation had turned to Jaime, to trying to get Kate to dish on what made her older brother blush.

So, Fletch still had a chance to flee.

"Fly, you fool," she hissed.

He grinned, bopped her on the nose. "Quiet, Gandalf." He shifted so he sat in the elephant of a chair next to her and took her hand before saying, "Need another bite of cookie? Or are you ready for me to introduce myself to your brothers?"

"Oh God," she moaned, and shoved the rest of the cookie into her mouth.

Fletch kissed her cheek then stood and while she was chewing—and couldn't protest—he rounded the table and started for her brothers. He was shaking Jaime's hand before she swallowed, then Brad stood and gave him a glare that should have withered Fletch's balls.

Everyone always thought Jaime was the one to watch out for because he was the oldest brother.

But it was Brad who was the most protective.

Brad might have traveled for many years, been out of the country more than in it, but he'd never missed important events, he'd always had his finger on the pulse of the family. He was the one to watch out for.

Fletcher seemed to pick up on that, too.

He extended a hand. "I'm Fletcher."

"Brad."

A clipped-out word.

"What makes you think that you're good enough to date my sister?"

Tammy swallowed the remnants of the cookie and winced, started to stand. Yeah, no. They weren't going to do this.

But Heidi beat her to it. "Bradley Huntington, can the toxic masculinity and sit your ass down, or I really *will* tell the entire table what I carry in my purse for you."

"Tammy can take care of herself," Kate said. Her eyes slanted toward Fletcher. "Not that we won't stab a bitch"— Tammy almost choked again, hearing Kate, who was the sweetest one in their bunch, calmly threaten Fletcher—"if you hurt her. But she'd probably beat us all to it."

Fletch glanced at her and winked, apparently not in the least bit put off by all the threatening. "I *know* she would."

She glugged down some of her margarita. "How do you deal with six of them?" she grumbled to Cora.

Her friend didn't miss a beat. "I moved across the country."

Tammy laughed. "Poor, poor baby."

"Damned right. *And* they scared off the latest guy I was dating when they visited. Now I have no one but me and my vibrator and you guys."

"Hopefully the vibrator is only put to use when you're *not* with us."

A wink. "Wouldn't you like to know?"

"Eww." But Tammy was grinning, and she'd relaxed enough that her gaze drifted away from Fletcher, who was now introducing himself to Tanner, and studied her friend whose expression was mischief personified in that moment. "Please, tell me you're joking."

"Dude. We've spent enough time together that I think you'd hear my panties vibrating, or at the very least know my O face." Cora drew her features into something so comical it should have been straight out of a choreographed Hollywood sex scene.

"I say again *ew*."

Cora grinned. "How're the nerves?"

Fletcher was chatting with Kate and Kels, and both women were clearly charmed. Jaime was watching him, but his expression was neutral, and she knew that Fletcher had probably already earned his approval, what with the cookie and his looking out for her. Brad would take a while, especially since she'd never brought a man home. He'd know that Fletcher was important and there would be extra consideration for that, which along with overprotectiveness, would mean that Fletch had some hoops to jump through.

But...Fletcher would.

Even though they were new, she understood that, *trusted* in that.

It was heels sailing into trees and carrying a cookie in his pocket for her.

It was gentle touches and kisses to her jaw and the soft way he said her name when he slid into her.

It was Fletcher and fake not being fake and his family and Trina.

Which was why she smiled at Cora, picked up her glass, and took a sip of her margarita. "The nerves are just fine."

TWENTY-TWO

Fletcher

ASIDE FROM BRAD shooting daggers at him the entire meal —they never did find out what was in his wife's purse—Fletcher had a great time hanging out with Tammy's friends.

They were a tight group, and though there were plenty of inside jokes—mostly about a show called *90 Day Fiancé: The Other Way*—he didn't feel isolated or on the outside during the couple of hours they sat around that table.

Tammy drank her margaritas, and pretty soon her embarrassed flush became an alcohol flush, but no one got sloppy.

It was Thursday, after all, and these people seemed to know their limits.

And not that he would be pressured to drink when he didn't want to—he had to drive Tammy home, after all—but he had an important meeting in the morning, so he didn't want to be off his game.

The meeting was key for him and his plans to talk his way into her bed every night.

He wanted forever.

So, he couldn't fuck it up.

They'd wrapped up dinner, ordering a final round of drinks and several more plates of sopapillas layered with honey and powdered sugar (and seriously, he needed to buy those items for his pantry and lick them off every inch of her body) because magically all of the alcohol and sticky, sugary desserts had been Hoovered. Then arguments had been made over paying the bill—apparently it was Tammy's turn to put the total on her credit card while everyone else Venmoed her, and her brothers didn't want her to have a big charge on her card.

To which she rolled her eyes, ignored them, handed her card to the waiter, and paid for dinner.

Everyone had sent her their share, and now they were all standing out front of the restaurant gabbing about work and life and Kate and Jaime's pets. Apparently, their goats had chewed their way through a fence in their back yard and had eaten their neighbor's prize-winning roses.

"Then Mrs. Davidson comes up to our porch, throws the stems at Jamie's feet, and declares, *This is war!*"

Jaime winced. "Never thought I would be terrified of an eighty-year-old woman."

"Well, she *did* have a cane," Kate pointed out.

"And was swinging it," Jaime muttered.

"Good thing you're excellent at dodging," Stef teased. "Gotta watch out for all those dangerous kitties."

"Hey, their nails are *sharp*," Jamie grumbled. "Plus, it's the roosters you have to watch out for."

"The Fuzz is an angel!" Kate protested. "He would never attack anyone with a cane."

"Only because he doesn't have opposable thumbs," Ben said quietly. The businessman, famous enough in tech circles that Fletch had recognized the man with just a glance, was quiet.

Not exactly standoffish, just more of an observer rather than joining in on the teasing.

So the quip made laughter bubble up in Fletcher's throat.

Tammy grinned up at him, kissed his jaw.

Kate—maybe one margarita too far into the evening—pointed her finger at Ben. "It's the quiet ones you have to watch out for."

"You'd know, Red," Jaime murmured, kissing the top of her head. "Come on, you two," he said to Brad and Heidi, who he was driving home. "I think talk of roosters and opposable thumbs means it's time for this one to go to bed."

"If there was ever a rooster who could manage to swing a cane at someone, it would be The Fuzz," Kate said, tossing her hands up.

Jaime chuckled, kissed her head again. "Of course, he would."

Stef snagged Ben's hand. "I have to stop by the lab on the way home, so we should probably go, too."

Kels, Tanner, and Cora all hung for a few more minutes, walking with Tammy and Fletcher toward their cars as they talked about the trip Kels and Tanner were planning for the following month and Cora's visit home in a couple of weeks for one of her brothers' weddings.

It was easy, and though he had friends here in town, they weren't like this.

There was a closeness that spoke of hours and hours together, of lives being intertwined and connected and over-lapping.

He loved that Tammy had that.

They reached his car—Tammy having taken a Lyft over because they were going back to her place afterward—and said goodbye to the others. Then they were inside and driving down the road, heading to Tammy's house.

She was quiet for a long time, and he thought that it might be the alcohol and all the food making her sleepy, but when she spoke, her voice wasn't sleepy in the least. "I hated him."

He frowned, glanced over at her. "Your brothers?"

Was it left over from growing up? From feeling like she was forgotten?

"No," she said. "I was jealous of them for a long time, of the attention my parents gave them and feeling like I was lost in the shuffle. But looking at it from the perspective of a grown up, of having someone I know sees me, I'm almost thankful for it." She fussed with the strap of the seat belt, running her fingers up and down the fabric. "It let me become my own person. Did it sting and hurt? Yes. Does it still hurt sometimes, and did I feel isolated? Of course."

"I'm sorry, honey," he said, "That must have been very hard."

"I'm not trying to say my parents weren't great," she said. "They were and are and it would probably break their hearts if they knew I felt this way, so I've never told them."

"Why not?"

A pause. "Why what?"

"Why haven't you told them?"

She went quiet again. "Did you not hear the part about breaking their hearts?"

"I heard it," he said, "but based on your brothers' planned disembowelment of me if I step a toe out of line, I know your family loves you, and I think it would kill them if they found out you were holding something this big back. I don't think they'd want you to be hurting when they could do something about it."

"I—" She blew out a breath. "I know it seems like a big thing," she whispered, "but it isn't."

He reached over the console and took her hand. "Isn't it?"

"I—" A sigh.

"You ran from relationships," he pointed out gently. "You said so yourself."

"I didn't run because of that. I—or not *only* that." She sighed again. "When I said I hate *him*, I meant Calvin. My ex. He's why I didn't want a relationship. He—I told him about my upbringing, about how I felt forgotten and on the outside. I gave him everything, every bit of vulnerability, and he said all the right things." She tightened her grip on his fingers. "I was really lost and feeling like I could never measure up to my siblings—" She huffed out a laugh. "I mean, have you meant them? They're ridiculously talented and my mom just runs a billion-dollar business like it's no big deal. It's hard to feel that I'm like them, that I fit in with them—"

He was even more glad for the meeting tomorrow.

"You're brilliant," he said. "There's a reason every project you submit gets approved, why people are clamoring to work with you."

A shrug. "It's just HR stuff."

He shook his head. "It's not just HR stuff. You're gathering important information so that our company, our *industry* can change for the better. Your work—our work—is critically valuable, and you're a huge part of that."

"Fletch," she began.

"Do you deny it's important?"

"I—" She pressed her lips together. "*No.* Making this kind of difference is what I've always wanted."

"Right." He turned into her driveway and parked. "Me, too. So," he said, reaching for her and taking her hands, "what did Calvin do?"

"It's not so much what he did—or not *solely* what he did." Tammy rolled her neck. "It's how I was with him."

He waited.

"We ran away together."

That was pretty much the last thing he expected her to say. "What do you mean, honey?"

Her eyes skated away from his. "I..." She blew out a breath and dropped her head back. "God, I was so stupid back then. I was eighteen. He was twenty. I thought he was amazing and my future, and I did a lot of stupid shit with him, not the least of which was giving him my virginity and then running off to get married without letting my family know."

Fuck.

"We went to Vegas. Got hitched, and then spent a month together. I told my family I was taking a road trip and needed the time alone before college. They...let me go. I was always independent, mostly because I'd had to be, you know?" She glanced at him and he nodded encouragingly. "So anyway, they were used to me going off and doing my own thing, didn't question when I disappeared for a while." She sighed. "And I was young and stupid and in love, so fucking excited to be taking that road trip with him, spending my days with a man who made me deliriously happy, feeling like he was the first person who wouldn't forget me." She sucked in a breath through her nose. "And all the while he was playing me. When he realized that he wasn't going to get handouts from my parents—because I didn't *get* handouts from them, and because I was determined to make my own way—he stole my car and left me on the side of the road in Wyoming."

"*What?*"

Fury had him flying out of his door, rounding the hood, and pulling her out of her seat. "Are you serious right now?"

She smiled sadly. "Ask me how terrifying it was to camp out overnight on the side of the road, nothing but twenty bucks in my pocket and knowing that grizzly bears were in the fucking forest around me."

He was going to kill Calvin.

He knew people. He could take the fucker down.

Okay, he didn't know people, but he was still going to take the fucker down.

"One second, we were arguing about money and how I wouldn't ask my parents for some so we could stay in some fancy hotel he wanted to spend the weekend in, and the next he was screeching to a stop on the side of the road, yanking me out so hard that I had sprained my wrist, ended up with scrapes on my elbows and arms and knees, a lump on my head." He wrapped an arm around her, led her to the house. "I woke up, tried to walk to town and ended up not making it that first night. I made it by the second, though, and filed a police report then called my parents. But I didn't tell them about Calvin, didn't tell *anyone* about the marriage. I just Googled annulments and figured out how to get myself out of it." She nibbled the corner of her mouth, her voice dropping to almost a whisper. "And then I never told anyone what really happened, just tried to shove it down and forget it, even as I promised myself I'd never make the same mistake again."

"Oh, babe."

He wrapped an arm around her, drew her toward the front door, punched the code to unlock it, and they went inside. "What happened to Calvin?"

She shook her head. "They found the car abandoned. The police never located him." He bypassed the living room, took her straight to the bedroom and sat her on the bed. Next step pajamas. He snagged them from the drawer, grabbed the ugly ass robe she'd worn that morning on her porch with the douchebag she'd been trying to get rid of. It was holey and faded, but it was also soft and warm, and she needed the comfort. "And anyway," she said, "I was determined to pretend it didn't happen. To forget that I'd been so critically stupid. Then then annulment went through, I locked everything down, and I made sure to never be in that position again."

"Hence the boyfriends—or lack thereof," he said, helping her get out of her work clothes and tugging on her pajamas. She smiled when he wrapped the robe around her.

"Yes. I wasn't going to ever do that again." Her nose wrinkled. "Until a stubborn as hell man was determined that I save the day for him." Her face softened. "He demanded that I ride in on my white stallion for him, so I did."

"And then he threw her shoes into the forest?"

"Pushy fucker, wasn't he?" she teased.

He laughed. "Damned right." He nudged her back, crawled into bed next to her, tugging her into his arms. "I'm really sorry that happened to you, baby." She nuzzled in. "What was Calvin's last name?"

"Why I—?" She stopped, shook her head. "I wasn't going to let my brothers get away with the big, tough man will solve my problems bullshit, and I'm certainly not going to let you do the same."

"Why not?"

She froze, then shot up, her mouth dropping open. "Fletcher, you—" Her words cut off when she presumably took in his expression—that being he was teasing her—and she shook her head. "You're in *so* much trouble."

"I know," he said. "Because I have a wonderful woman with a beautiful heart in my life who is so fucking brave and strong and smart, and I would do anything for her."

Her face went soft.

"But, sweetheart," he told her gently, "that wonderful, brave woman needs to talk to her family about this."

Soft to panicked in a heartbeat.

"I know it's scary," he said, gently stroking her hair back. "I know you've held it in, and that you were trying to push it down so you didn't have to deal with it, so that you could move on. And as a man who was great at doing that, at wanting to pretend I was over Trina and then thought a fake relationship was the solution to my problems—which, luckily for me, turned out for the better—I know that's not the way forward. So, I'm not telling you to talk to your family, I'm just...I don't know...*suggesting* strongly that you get this—Calvin, feeling like an outsider—off your chest, baby. Then we can move forward and conquer all the HR reports, change the face of the industry, and you can slum it by dating a guy who's sort of at your level."

Her brows pulled together. Her lips pursed. But her eyes were filled with love, and that was enough for him. "I'll take it under advisement."

A kiss to the tip of her nose. "That's good enough for me."

She smiled. "And I'm slumming it?"

"Definitely."

Tammy rolled her eyes. "Did you forget that you carry a chocolate chip cookie in your pocket? That you got mad at my shoes for having the audacity to hurt my feet?"

He grinned. "I'm never going to hear the end of the shoes, am I?"

"Nope." She pressed a kiss to his mouth. "And the reason I can tease you about the shoes is because I know I'm safe. With you, Fletch, I know I'm safe, know I'm seen."

His heart squeezed tight.

And he hoped she also knew she was loved.

Soon.

When they were together a little longer. When it wasn't so new and fresh, he would tell one Tammy Huntington that she'd stolen his heart.

And hope she would trust him with hers right back.

TWENTY-THREE

Tammy

THREE WEEKS, THREE FRIENDS' dinners, one weekend with Fletch's parents, and two Huntington-McLeod (Kate and her family were a hoot, and it wasn't terrible that she got to see Heidi, too) dinners later, Tammy was finalizing the last lines of the first report for her diversity project. They'd conducted some stealthy research, seeing how different email signatures—male versus female, standard English names versus some that were more unfamiliar—were communicated with.

Each reply was then evaluated on a scale they'd set up beforehand and that rating was put into a program to be tracked.

Now they had all the ratings and the replies and the report she'd just finished putting together was going to be sent over to CEO Heather O'Keith.

It was going to be awesome.

Maybe as awesome as dinner the next night.

A King-McLeod-Huntington family BBQ was happening at Kate's house.

Three families. Numerous couples. Several goats and The

Fuzz. It was going to be total chaos. But finally, all the moms were going to meet. Tammy had absolute confidence that Connie was going to join the ranks of The Moms, and the ultimate ruling power of the universe would become a trifecta.

A scary thought.

She grinned. It was going to be wonderful.

Because she was *in love!*

She spun in her chair, catching a glimpse of the skyline of San Francisco through the window as her chair turned, absolutely giddy that she was dating Fletcher, that not one moment of it hadn't been amazing, that there was no drama or doubts.

Every night they'd been together.

Every day they ate lunch together.

And though they'd played it relatively cool at work, there wasn't anyone in the department who didn't know they were together. Mostly because Lisa had been moaning about them making Lovey Eyes at each other. But really...it was because they were making Lovey Eyes at each other.

She sighed happily and spun once again.

Then nearly flew out of her chair when she heard, "Here." Lisa smacked down a file on her desk, and Tammy barely got her feet on the floor before her boss was striding out of her office, muttering about young love.

"Make sure you give *your* young love a kiss when you get home, Lis," she called.

Her boss flipped her off over her shoulder—which was normal. She was cranky and grumpy and despite the HR distinction—they were sometimes the worst offenders when it came to proper behavior—or at least with cursing and flipping the bird. But what happened next wasn't normal. Because Lisa spun around, and her face was sad.

Damned sad.

"I hope he's worth it," she said. "I hope to God Fletcher is worth giving everything up."

"Wh—"

But before she could finish the question, Lisa was gone, shutting the door behind her, leaving Tammy in stunned silence for a long moment before she remembered the file.

"What the fuck?" she whispered, reaching for the envelope.

Tearing it open.

Whispering again, "What the fuck?"

As the bottom dropped out of her world.

TWENTY-FOUR

Fletcher

HE'D LEFT work early to get everything ready.

His parents would be in early tomorrow morning, so he wanted this night with Tammy to be special and romantic and just about them.

He loved his family and hers was awesome, too.

But tonight, he had Tammy in his house, his bed, and it was going to be an awesome night.

There was a knock at the door, which he thought was weird, but then again, he suffered from Amazonesia, so it could easily be just a package showing up magically on his porch. Straightening the bouquet of red-tinged sunflowers he'd picked up to celebrate their favorite flower, he headed to answer the door.

Tammy was on the other side.

He felt his smile grow. "Hey, sweetheart," he said, reaching for her, "did you forget your key—"

She stepped back.

Her face went cold.

Frost slid down his spine. "Tammy, honey, what is it?"

She slapped a folder to his chest. "How could you?" she hissed. "How could you do this to me?"

He barely caught the papers before they dropped to the ground. "What is this?" he asked, shifting the file to one hand, reaching out with the other to grab her arm when she started to turn away from him, to try and stride away across the porch. "Wait, Tammy. Seriously, what's going on?"

She yanked her arm out of his grip. "Don't fucking touch me. I trusted you. I *loved* you. I put my fear aside and gave you everything I had in me, and y-you fucked me over." A shaky breath, tears pouring down her cheeks. "I thought Calvin had destroyed me, but you...you incinerated me, my heart, my dreams, my j-job—"

"Tam—" He started to step toward her, but she backed away again.

"Don't—"

"Talk to me, sweetheart. Tell me—"

A shake of her head. "No. *No*, I'm not doing this. You—you —" More tears escaped. And then she turned and ran down the steps, sprinting for her car.

"Tammy, wait!" He started to take off after her, but then remembered what he held. He flipped open the top of the envelope, pulled out the papers, and started to read. His heart sank down to his feet as he began to process the words, dread scorching through him. This was wrong. This wasn't what they'd discussed. Every bit of it was wrong. So *fucking* wrong. "Tam—"

Tires squealed in his driveway, and his head jerked up, gaze going to her car—or rather watching her car shoot away from his house like the hounds of hell were after her.

Or maybe like an asshole had broken her heart.

Again.

"Fuck," he whispered, turning and striding into the house.

The sunflowers on the counter mocked him.

"Fuck!" He growled, shoving his feet into his boots, wanting to put a fist through the wall, wanting to tear up the papers in his hands or light them on fire, to turn them to ash and pretend this hadn't just happened.

But it had.

And he needed to find a way to fix it.

Heather O'Keith was a scary motherfucker.

Probably because he'd just stormed into her office, bypassing the desk that normally held a secretary preventing just this sort of interaction.

But then again, it was nearly seven on a Friday evening and most sane people weren't in the office.

Heather wasn't always considered sane—or at least in business circles—mostly because she pulled insane hours. Workaholic was a weak description for her. Though, rumor had it her husband Clay Steele had chilled out her working habits, at least a little bit. She took time off, and more often than not, she wouldn't be here this late, especially on a Friday.

But he'd known she would be in.

She'd just returned from overseeing the testing on Robo-Tech's drone project, a collaboration with the Scottish billionaire, Colin McGregor. Fletcher's understanding was that it would be utilized to drop food and medical supplies in areas hard-hit by natural—or man-made—disasters or those places not easily accessible to relief workers. The whole project sounded pretty fucking amazing, and normally he'd be proud to be part of a company that was investing in that kind of humanitarian project.

What *didn't* sound amazing was that he'd had a meeting

with the head of HR and Heather O'Keith three fucking weeks ago where he'd discussed his and Tammy's relationship and requested that he be the one to be transferred out of Lisa's department.

He was supposed to be taking a slight demotion, even.

Tammy—God, *Tammy* was supposed to be untouched, unaffected, not to have her position change in the slightest.

Because it was her dream, and he would never take it away.

"We had a fucking *arrangement*," he snapped, trying to hold on to his temper, because this was his livelihood, but also struggling with control because he was pissed out of his mind. He'd done the right thing, gone along the right channels. HR had brought in Heather because it was an unusual request and though she'd wanted some assurance that this was the right thing for him as her employee, she'd told him that she respected his decision.

And then *this*.

Tammy being shifted out of HR.

Completely out. She'd been so fucking excited to finish her report, so excited to share the results with Lisa, with Demi (the head of HR), with Heather.

And instead, she got a shitty ass letter telling her that she was being transferred to engineering.

Engineering?

Seriously, what the fuck was that?

Her specialty was HR.

Her *dream* was HR.

Put *him* in fucking Engineering.

"Careful," Clay said, who was a regular enough visitor at the office that Fletcher recognized Heather's husband. Well, that and the fact that he'd been kissing Heather when Fletcher had stormed into her office would have clued him in. Either way, Clay wasn't looking all that pleased at the interruption.

"Fuck careful," Fletcher snapped, stomping over to Heather's desk and slamming the file onto the messy surface.

And yeah, interrupting his boss and her husband in an interlude and snapping at both of them was probably stupid as fuck, especially if he wanted to keep his job—or get Tammy back her old one.

"Sit the fuck down," Heather said, picking up the envelope and opening it.

Fletcher moved to the chair but didn't sit down, just gripped the back of it, his fingers digging into the wood. "You assured me that everything was going to be okay. You *promised* me that Tammy would be taken care of."

Heather's eyes flicked across the papers. "It seems like she's been taken care of," she said. "Same level. Same salary. In fact, a better opportunity for growth."

"A different job description," he growled. "One that won't have her doing what she's passionate about."

"Hmm." Heather settled into her chair as she continued to read. Clay remained standing—and glaring at Fletcher. She set the file down, glanced at her computer screen. Then she picked up the phone and made a call that had his heart dropping all over again.

"Security?" she said, "I need you to..."

TWENTY-FIVE

Tammy

HER EYES WERE SWOLLEN.

She could actually feel them pulsing in her skull, and her throat felt like shit.

She'd barely made it back to her house, her tears had been streaming down her face, clouding her vision.

Fucking hell.

Then she'd sat in her driveway, unable to go in, the betrayal pulsing through her.

Anger taking over.

Her tears drying.

She'd found herself backing out and driving aimlessly.

Until she'd parked in a familiar lot.

Bright lights, empty parking spaces surrounding her.

A multi-story building in front of her. It was mostly dark inside, pretty much anyone with a life having already gone home for the weekend. She still grabbed her keys and her badge.

Not picked.

Forgotten.

Those two sentiments rattled around her brain, and she let herself in and headed for the elevator, up to her floor. To the HR department. To her office.

To the report still sitting on her desk.

Because she was going to go through it one more time. She was going to make it the best fucking report anyone had ever seen.

And then she was going to look for another job.

Because *she* wanted to be the one who was picked.

Not the one who was shuffled around because someone else —because Fletcher—was more important. Not again. No more.

No—

"Ma'am?"

She blinked, halting in the process of opening her office door, and turned to see a security guard was standing in the hall, his arms crossed. "Y-yes?" she asked haltingly.

"I need you to come with me."

"I—" She held up her badge. "I work here."

"You need to come with me."

"I just want to get a report—"

"You need to come with me."

Seriously?

Maybe the icing on the cake was that she was getting fired. Not just a position shift. But canned right when she felt like she was going to live out her dreams.

Because she'd let a fucking man in.

That protective bubble surrounding her had popped—had disappeared like it never existed in the first place.

She sighed, closed the door. "Okay," she said on a sigh, "Lead the way." And she followed the guard to and the into the elevator.

Kick her out of the building.

Send her off to the police.

Book and fingerprint her. Throw her in a cell. Do whatever they did to people who snuck in to do extra work on a Friday night.

Yes, she was being dramatic.

But fuck...Fletcher. He'd done this and—

The elevator doors opened, and she stepped off.

Then looked around in confusion. This wasn't the lobby. This was...the executive level. What the fuck?

The guard touched her elbow. "This way."

Dread settled into her, a stifling cloud, but she was on the floor, and she'd gotten the file with her new job in it. If that wasn't on the table any longer, if Heather O'Keith or some other executive wanted to demote her in person, well, then Tammy was about to get demoted—or hell, maybe even fired—in person.

The guard led her all the way down the hall, past the smaller offices, and to the one directly at the end.

Oh, joy.

Yup.

Tammy was about to see Heather O'Keith in person.

On a Friday night. Probably with her mascara running all over the place, her voice hoarse from her sobs, her eyes swollen.

Yay.

The guard opened the door, nudged her inside.

The moment Tammy saw who was within, she tried to turn and GTFO. But then the door *clicked* closed behind her.

And she was shut in Heather O'Keith's office with a man she never wanted to see again.

For the record, that man wasn't Clay Steele, the handsome blue-eyed man standing with his arms crossed behind Heather's chair, but rather the handsome blue-eyed man who'd held her heart...and then shattered it.

She spun, intending to flee.

Yes, it was cowardly.

But fuck, this *sucked*.

"Sit," Heather ordered.

"I—"

"Tammy. *Sit.*"

Ah fuck, that *tone*. It was Mom Tone or Boss Tone or Mom-Boss Tone.

Whatever it was, she found herself unable to ignore it. She found herself walking toward the chair and plunking her ass down into it.

And then waiting.

As Heather studied her and didn't say anything. And seriously, was *this* what they were doing here? Sitting in silence while Tammy's heart broke all over again?

The quiet stretched on, tense and still. Heather's eyes on hers. Fletcher a silent, antsy presence to her right. "I—"

"Fletcher met with me and Demi almost three weeks ago," Heather began before Tammy's sentence could materialize. "He disclosed your relationship and requested that he be transferred out from Lisa's department so that you could stay in your position. He was going to take a demotion so that your job description didn't change."

What?

But the question stayed in her throat, smothered by too many emotions bursting through her, a firework of hope, of pain, of longing and joy and fury.

Still, her eyes shot to Fletcher's.

He nodded, barely.

"Now, what I didn't tell him. Or you," she added when Tammy's gaze moved back to the CEO, "was that Fletcher taking a demotion just so we could hop through some HR loops didn't sit well with me. You weren't a direct report to him. There was no power disparity. If he was in Lisa's position, that would present some difficulty." Heather sighed and leaned back in her chair, steepling her fingers. "But he's not. And while he has more seniority than you, it's not enough to manifest into the issue that Lisa was so worried about."

Fletcher shifted closer.

Heather continued talking. "So, he left the meeting thinking his demotion would be happening. He'd signed the paperwork, filed everything he needed to file. But I pulled his papers before Demi could process them. Because I got wind of the project you"—she held Tammy's gaze—"were spearheading. I was excited. This is exactly the type of project I wanted to conduct when I took over RoboTech. What you're doing is meaningful and important, but truthfully, it's a better fit with the engineering department. They have the programming and data analysis experience. In fact, even though I've only seen the preliminaries for what you're doing, I think it'll mesh perfectly with the program Kelsey Scott's team is developing."

Tammy froze. "Kels?" Her friend, Kels?

Heather's face gentled slightly. "Yes, *Kels*." She stood, rounded her desk, and sat on the edge of it. "You'd be okay working with her? Doing more of what you're doing now, just in a different department?"

A bit dumbfounded, a lot relieved, and with excitement beginning to brew, Tammy nodded.

"Good." Heather sighed. "So, now I find myself in a position I hate: having to apologize."

Clay snorted.

Heather shot him a glare then turned back to her and Fletch. "As much as I don't appreciate someone"—her eyes locked onto Fletcher—"barreling into my office and demanding that I fix this. I also *really* don't like it when I fuck up. I planned on talking to you about the job next week when I was back in the office, not at seven at night on a Friday."

Tammy winced.

"However, what I didn't plan on was my very efficient assistant being three steps ahead of me and filing the paperwork before I had a chance to discuss it with you."

"I—" Tammy sucked in a breath and released it slowly. "So, I'm really not getting demoted?"

"No, Huntington," Heather said with a smile. "I want you to keep doing what you've been doing, just on a bigger scale."

"And—" Her gaze went to Fletcher's. "You really were going to take a demotion for me?"

His face gentled. "In a heartbeat, baby."

That protective bubble reappeared without warning, surrounding her in a flash, making her wonder if it had ever been gone, or if it had just been invisible. Because she was a fucking moron. She groaned, dropped her head into her hands. "I'm such an idiot."

Warm palms on her face, lips brushing her forehead. "Not an idiot. Understandably upset."

"I stormed to your house and tossed papers in your face," she snapped. "Then stormed off without even getting an explanation from you. So *fucking* stupid. I should have let you explain and—*oof.*" One second, she was in the chair and the next she was in his arms.

"Tammy, honey," he said, "If I'd gotten this news without an explanation, I would have freaked, too." He stroked a hand down her back. "This is a trigger for you. You need trust and care and not to have any secrets, and your job is important to you. Do I wish you would have given me a second to have a conversation about this? To read the paperwork? Of course." His hand stroked back up. "But would I have still stormed in here and interrupted Heather and Clay canoodling?"

"Canood—"

She cut off the question, remembering where they were.

In her boss's boss's *boss's* office.

Shit.

She flew out of Fletcher's arms, gaze darting around the office, realizing that she and Fletch were alone.

"They were canoodling?" she whispered, half-expecting them to pop out from some secret hidey hole and tell her and Fletcher to stop with *their* canoodling.

He nodded. "Jumped apart like guilty school kids." His mouth turned up. "Kind of like what you just did."

She found herself chuckling...and then she found herself crumbling.

More tears.

But these ones were tears of relief.

It didn't matter, though, because the tears had barely cleared her lashes when she was in Fletcher's arms again, his arms stroking up and down her back, his words gentle and sweet. "I can't believe you stormed into our boss's boss's *boss's* office going to bat for me," she said when she could finally speak again without losing it.

"I'd do it again."

No hesitation.

No prevarication.

Her heart swelled.

Because she knew that, too.

"I'm sorry," she whispered guilt practically drowning her.

"I'm not."

Again, no hesitation. No prevarication. Just truth.

"Why?"

He stroked her cheek. "Because now you get to live out your even bigger dream.

"Oh, fuck."

Fletch went still. "What?"

"You know you've gone and made me fall in love with you?"

Somehow, he went even more still. "What?" he breathed.

She brushed her nose along his. "You heard me. How can I not love a man who throws my shoes into trees?" A smile on his gorgeous mouth. "How can I not love a man who has a favorite flower?" A kiss to those gorgeous lips—one that left her breathless, her heart racing. "How can I not *love* a man who wants to make my dreams come true?"

Even though she'd stupidly lost it on him.

Even though she'd run.

He'd still fought for her, for her dreams.

That meant more than anything else.

"Tammy," he whispered, and his throat was clogged with tears, his eyes shiny. "Fuck, I love you."

She smiled, those words strengthening the bubble, running rebar all along the inside, making it so it would never pop, never collapse.

Safe.

She was safe.

And in love.

Tammy Huntington, the woman who promised a hundred, a thousand times that she would never, *ever* trust her heart to another person, had freely given it away.

Wasn't it fucking great?

EPILOGUE

Fletcher, a month later

"AND I KNOW I should have talked to you about this sooner..." Tammy trailed off, tears glistening on her cheeks. She'd just told her mom everything about Calvin, about feeling forgotten growing up, and how those had played into her avoiding relationships with men.

"Oh, honey," Tawny said, sliding closer on the couch and hugging her daughter close. "I do wish you'd told me sooner, but I understand why you might have held that in."

"You do?"

Tawny smoothed back Tammy's hair, wiped her tears. "I should have seen through the shields, baby. You were always so independent, but I never considered that you felt that you had to be." A kiss to Tammy's forehead. "I'm so sorry."

"No. Don't apologize. It's not your fault—"

"Honey." Andrew's voice took on a sharp edge as he joined his wife and daughter on the couch. "Who's the parent in this scenario?"

"But—"

"We *should* have noticed."

Andrew slipped an arm around both of them, held them close, and Fletcher decided that was the cue for him to leave. Quietly, he stood from the armchair Tammy had asked him to sit in for moral, and left the room on soft feet.

They needed privacy and to talk it out more.

Not that one conversation would fix everything.

But it would be a start, and Tammy hopefully would feel heard and seen and like a weight had been lifted off her shoulders.

"You love her."

He turned at the cold voice, turned to face the one Huntington who'd continued to glare at him over the last months during every friends' dinner, every time their families got together, every single time that he and Brad were in the same room.

Now, it was still cold.

But there was something else in that tonight.

"That's not even a question," Fletcher said, moving down the hall and away from the conversation that was taking place in the living room. He didn't want to distract Tammy or her parents from what they needed to talk out, not when they finally *were* talking it out.

Not when his beautiful, kind Tammy had finally found the strength to share.

The demons wouldn't have any power over her.

He was still working on finding out Calvin's last name from her, determined to do...*something* to make the other man pay.

But considering that Tammy was the only woman he'd ever met who was more stubborn than he was, Fletcher didn't have much hope that he'd get it out of her.

"Who was he?"

Fletch stopped and faced Tammy's brother. "What?"

"The man who hurt her?"

Fletcher glanced back down the hall, wanting to make sure they were far enough away from Tammy and her parents. "Who says a man hurt her?"

"*I'm* saying that." Brad stepped closer, his expression so like Tammy's that it was uncanny. "Tell me so I can take care of it."

It was tempting to admit what he knew, to get an ally in the Fuck Calvin Up plan. But this was Tammy's truth, and she'd just found the courage to share it with her parents. It needed to be on her terms to share it with her siblings.

"And *I'm* saying that your sister has it handled, and you need to back off. She'll come to you if she needs help."

Silence.

Tense silence and flashing eyes.

But he'd been on the other end of that Huntington glare plenty of times before.

He knew how to withstand it.

He just held Brad's eyes and said again, "This is Tammy's life, and I'm supporting her in it, not taking it over."

"That's bull—"

"*That's,*" Heidi interrupted, "perfectly reasonable, and you know it, love. Your sister is perfectly capable of handling her own life." She swept into the hall and wove her arm through Brad's. "Come on. We're heating up the pizza oven, and you need to choose your toppings." She started to tug her husband toward the backyard, but glanced over her shoulder. "For the record, Fletcher, that was the perfect answer. Tammy doesn't need a keeper, or a protector. She needs someone who loves her for the awesome woman she is."

Brad scowled. "The man threw her expensive *heels* into the forest."

God. He really never *was* going to hear the end of the shoes.

"That was sweet," Heidi said. "That just shows how much he loves her."

"So is sharing the name of the asshole who hurt her," Brad grumbled.

"Someone hurt her?" Heidi dropped her husband's arm and marched over to Fletcher. "You didn't tell me that someone hurt her. Tell me the asshole's name and I'll—"

"I love her for the capable, strong woman she is," he said. "And I would never take away her ability to take over." A beat. "Even if I've begged her to let me." Brad finally lost the fury, the first notes of humor entering his eyes. "I would take the burden if I could. But I can't in this instance. She doesn't want me to, so I have to respect that."

"And you're just going to step back and accept that?" Brad asked.

"I love her," Fletcher said. "There's nothing *but* acceptance."

Brad held his gaze for a long time before nodding, and there might have been approval in Tammy's brother's eyes.

Might have been.

Or maybe that was wishful thinking.

Or maybe not.

Because Brad clapped him on the shoulder and started walking again, heading for the sliding glass doors that led to the back yard and the pizza oven that was warmed up and ready to create deliciousness.

"Come on," Brad said before he went out. "Let's eat."

"Wait." Heidi stopped in the hall, glancing between them. "You said that someone hurt Tammy. Who is he?" She whipped out her phone, started taking notes. "What's his full name and occupation?" she asked, fingers flying. "Oh, and his social security number."

"Heid—" Brad began.

"Dish, King," she snapped. "Now."

"What happened to Tammy being capable of handling her own shit?"

"What *happened* is someone hurt my Tammy and I'm going to—"

"Do nothing because it's in the past?"

Tammy's voice slid through the hall, and they froze. Gut clenching, Fletcher turned to see her standing behind them, her parents close. All three of them had reddened eyes, but one look into Tammy's told him that she was okay, that while not everything was solved with just that one conversation, this was a step forward.

Tawny nodded at him, Andrew following suit, his expression approving.

Whether that was for sparking the conversation between them, or because of what he'd said just now, he didn't know. He didn't care either.

Tammy looked lighter and happier, despite the red eyes.

And that was the only thing that mattered to him.

Fletcher smiled. "Hi, sweetheart."

"Hi," she whispered.

She moved toward him, threw herself into his arms. "I love you."

"I will *never* grow tired of hearing you say that."

A pert smile. "Me neither."

He took the hint. "I love you too, Tammy Huntington. From the first moment I laid eyes on you, until the time comes that my lids slide closed for the last time. You're here"—he tapped the spot above his heart—"and I'm never *ever* going to stop seeing you."

"Dammit, Fletcher."

"What?" he asked.

But he knew, knew that tone, knew that curse, knew why she got so stiff.

Emotions.

Free of concrete and barbed wire. Out in the open.

Trusted to him.

And he wouldn't let her down, couldn't bear to *ever* let her down.

So, he just tugged her against his chest, wrapped his arms around her, and when she'd finished crying, wiped away her tears. The hall got mysteriously empty, her breathing slowed.

Then his strong, capable, love of his life stepped out of the circle of his arms.

Took his hand.

Tugged him toward the group of people who loved her, who wouldn't forget her, who would *see* her.

Always.

Because he wouldn't allow it to be any other way.

BAD BEST FRIEND

Cora

CHEETOS WERE REALLY the best thing on the planet.

Okay, maybe not the *best* thing.

Because she *could* list a few things that were better than the faux cheese crunchy deliciousness—those being her mom's chocolate pecan pie, the croissants from Molly's in her new hometown (San Francisco had a lot of perks compared to the small suburban city that she had grown up in, not the least of which were the delicious treats from her favorite bakery), and sitting at home in her fuzziest socks while watching the Hallmark channel on repeat.

Those were all better than Cheetos.

But truly, they we all a close second.

Which was mostly because she had her bag of chips propped on the couch next to her, her orange powered-covered fingers—on her left hand, always, because the right hand was for the remote so that she could pause to sigh heartfeltly at all the perfect parts. And to rewind and watch them again.

And to sigh again.

She also had a box with baked goods on her coffee table—minus one croissant because she couldn't wait until the morning —and hell, why should she? It was Friday night. She was single because her brothers had decided to chase off the last man she'd dated.

Truthfully, she couldn't complain too much.

Six brothers was a lot of testosterone, and when they got it in their heads that she needed protecting, it was nearly impossible to get them to stop.

They were dogs to a bone.

Mostly because they had been protecting her almost her whole life.

Five. She'd been five years old when her dad died. The youngest. The baby. The long-awaited girl after *all* those boys. To be protected. Coddled. Looked-out for. It was sweet, but stifling. Loving, but overbearing. Coming from a genuine place, but sometimes so absolutely infuriating that she wanted to tear her hair out.

Her older brothers had made it their full-time jobs—complete with benefits, plenty of PTO, and 401k plans—to watch over her.

Because her dad had ingrained it in them.

Her dad, who she loved...but—she sighed—she just wished she had the memories her brothers did, her mom did.

Everything she had was blurry on the edges, more feelings and smells than crystal clear memories.

Being tossed up in the air, flying so high, feeling like she could touch the sky.

The smell of his skin, his hair.

The feel of his strong arms hugging me tight.

It was enough...and it wasn't *nearly* enough. She wanted what they had, but knew she would never get it. So she contented herself with the stories, and pushed the longing she felt for all that she'd missed out on deep, deep down.

So many people had it worse.

She could suck up her daddy issues, be grateful her her family, even for the big lugs that seemed determined to mess up her love life, and enjoy her Cheetos and Hallmark.

"Exactly, Cor," she whispered to herself. "Cheetos. Croissants. Forests in Vermont where small town girls find their happy endings with lumberjacks who had thick, bushy beards and plaid shirts that threatened to burst from the sheer size of their biceps."

Pleased with herself, she nodded, hit play on the remote and started to get wrapped up in the story—and God, seriously, those colorful leaves were *gorgeous*—thinking that she really needed to plan a trip to Vermont when there was a knock at her door.

Sighing, she paused her movie, wiped her Cheeto fingers on the napkin she had draped over her leg for just for that purpose, and stood.

A glance through the peephole had her sighing again, this time paired with shaking her head.

She tugged open the door.

"Rafe," she grumbled, "which of my brothers sent you?"

She had six brothers, but she might as well have a seventh because Rafe had hung around Jeremy, Wyatt, and Asher—her eldest three brothers who were all within three years of each other (her poor mother)—all the way through elementary, middle, and high school and well into adulthood.

Case in point, he just shrugged, barged into her house, and said, "All of them."

She muttered an epithet, closed the door behind him, and hurried past him, lest he try to steal her croissants.

With six brothers, she'd learned to protect what was really important.

Which was why she grabbed the bag of Cheetos right after she'd safely secured the box of pastries.

He dropped a bag on the floor—right in the middle of her living room—and sank onto the couch, picking up the remote and changing the channel, like he'd visited a hundred times before.

And she supposed he had.

He always seemed to tag along.

To *protect* her.

And yes, she was mentally doing air quotes to go along with that thought, even as she shoved his feet off the coffee table. "What are you doing here, Rafe?" she asked, snatching the remote back, and returning the television to its rightful place—the Hallmark channel.

But she didn't get to rewind the movie back to where she'd left off.

Because Rafe shrugged his bulky shoulders, nodded at the bag, and said—

"I'm moving in."

—Bad Best Friend coming March 1st, 2022

BAD BEST FRIEND

Cora and Rafe's story is coming March 1st, 2021!
Preorder your copy at www.books2read.com/BadBestFriend

Hate missing Elise's new releases? Love contests, exclusive excerpts and giveaways?

Then signup for Elise's newsletter here!

http://eepurl.com/bdnmEj

BILLIONAIRE'S CLUB

Bad Night Stand

Bad Breakup

Bad Husband

Bad Hookup

Bad Divorce

Bad Fiancé

Bad Boyfriend

Bad Blind Date

Bad Wedding

Bad Engagement

Bad Bridesmaid

Bad Swipe

Bad Girlfriend

Bad Best Friend

ALSO BY ELISE FABER

Billionaire's Club **(all stand alone)**

Bad Night Stand

Bad Breakup

Bad Husband

Bad Hookup

Bad Divorce

Bad Fiancé

Bad Boyfriend

Bad Blind Date

Bad Wedding

Bad Engagement

Bad Bridesmaid

Bad Swipe

Bad Girlfriend

Gold Hockey **(all stand alone)**

Blocked

Backhand

Boarding

Benched

Breakaway

Breakout

Checked

Coasting

Centered

Charging

Caged

Crashed

Cycled

Breakers Hockey (**all stand alone**)

Broken

Boldly

Breathless

KTS Series

Riding The Edge

Crossing The Line

Leveling The Field

Scorching The Earth

Love, Action, Camera (all stand alone)

Dotted Line

Action Shot

Close-Up

End Scene

Meet Cute

Love After Midnight (**all stand alone**)

Rum And Notes

Virgin Daiquiri

On The Rocks

Sex On The Seats

Life Sucks Series (all stand alone)

Train Wreck

Hot Mess

Dumpster Fire

Clusterf*@k

FUBAR

Roosevelt Ranch Series (all stand alone, series complete)

Disaster at Roosevelt Ranch

Heartbreak at Roosevelt Ranch

Collision at Roosevelt Ranch

Regret at Roosevelt Ranch

Desire at Roosevelt Ranch

Phoenix Series (read in order)

Phoenix Rising

Dark Phoenix

Phoenix Freed

Phoenix: LexTal Chronicles (rereleasing soon, stand alone, Phoenix world)

From Ashes

In Flames

To Smoke

Stand Alones

Someday, Maybe (YA)

ABOUT THE AUTHOR

USA Today bestselling author, Elise Faber, loves chocolate, Star Wars, Harry Potter, and hockey (the order depending on the day and how well her team -- the Sharks! -- are playing). She and her husband also play as much hockey as they can squeeze into their schedules, so much so that their typical date night is spent on the ice. Elise changes her hair color more often than some people change their socks, loves sparkly things, and is the mom to two exuberant boys. She lives in Northern California. Connect with her in her Facebook group, the Fabinators or find more information about her books at www.elisefaber.com.

f facebook.com/elisefaberauthor

a amazon.com/author/elisefaber

BB bookbub.com/profile/elise-faber

instagram.com/elisefaber

g goodreads.com/elisefaber

pinterest.com/elisefaberwrite